P9-BZI-072

"If he's back, he'll come for me." Rachel spoke the words with certainty.

"Then he'll have to get *through* me," Dylan fired back, unable to hold those words inside any longer.

Her eyes widened.

He put his hands on her. He *had* to touch her. His fingers curled around her slender shoulders. "He isn't going to have the chance to hurt you. I'll stop him. I'll do anything necessary in order to make sure he doesn't have the chance to get to you again."

"And what am I supposed to do?" Her body brushed against his. "Hide? Stay in the shadows while you hunt? That's not who I am, Dylan. You know that."

He did. He knew everything about her.

EVIDENCE OF PASSION

New York Times Bestselling Author
CYNTHIA EDEN

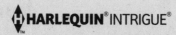

HARLEQUIN® INTRIGUE®

If you purchased this book without a cover you should be aware
that this book is stolen property. It was reported as "unsold and
destroyed" to the publisher, and neither the author nor the
publisher has received any payment for this "stripped book."

Recycling programs
for this product may
not exist in your area.

Thank you so much to all of the readers who
have supported my Shadow Agents. I hope that
you enjoy the latest installment in the series.

And thank you to the wonderful team at
Harlequin—it is always a pleasure!

ISBN-13: 978-0-373-69777-9

EVIDENCE OF PASSION

Copyright © 2014 by Cindy Roussos

All rights reserved. Except for use in any review, the reproduction or
utilization of this work in whole or in part in any form by any electronic,
mechanical or other means, now known or hereafter invented, including
xerography, photocopying and recording, or in any information storage
or retrieval system, is forbidden without the written permission of the
publisher, Harlequin Enterprises Limited, 225 Duncan Mill Road,
Don Mills, Ontario M3B 3K9, Canada.

This is a work of fiction. Names, characters, places and incidents are
either the product of the author's imagination or are used fictitiously,
and any resemblance to actual persons, living or dead, business
establishments, events or locales is entirely coincidental.

This edition published by arrangement with Harlequin Books S.A.

For questions and comments about the quality of this book,
please contact us at CustomerService@Harlequin.com.

® and TM are trademarks of Harlequin Enterprises Limited or its
corporate affiliates. Trademarks indicated with ® are registered in the
United States Patent and Trademark Office, the Canadian Intellectual
Property Office and in other countries.

Printed in U.S.A.

ABOUT THE AUTHOR

New York Times and *USA TODAY* bestselling author Cynthia Eden writes tales of romantic suspense and paranormal romance. Her books have received starred reviews from *Publishers Weekly,* and she has received a RITA® Award nomination for best romantic suspense novel. Cynthia lives in the Deep South, loves horror movies and has an addiction to chocolate. More information about Cynthia may be found on her website, www.cynthiaeden.com, or you can follow her on Twitter (www.twitter.com/cynthiaeden).

Books by Cynthia Eden

HARLEQUIN INTRIGUE

CAST OF CHARACTERS

Rachel Mancini—An ex-lawyer, Rachel now spends her days and nights working for the Elite Operations Division. The scars from Rachel's past haunt her but she is determined to move forward with her life...until the nightmare from her past rises up to strike out at her again.

Dylan Foxx—Once a SEAL, always a SEAL... Dylan Foxx is the team leader at the EOD. He is always alert for danger—and always on guard. When a killer targets Rachel, Dylan knows that he will do everything within his power to protect her. But he's not just protecting Rachel because she's part of his team. He's staying close to her because Dylan knows he can't live without her....

Thomas Anthony—Thomas Anthony is a man with secrets. A martial arts expert with a dark past, Thomas is supposed to be part of the EOD team. But can he be trusted? Danger lurks just beneath his surface, and Thomas is working his own hidden agenda.

Noelle Evers—As an FBI profiler, Noelle's job is to help locate and track down the most dangerous criminals out there. But when the danger seems to be coming from within the EOD, Noelle has to figure out just who can be trusted...and who should be feared.

Bruce Mercer—The director of the EOD, Bruce Mercer must often make difficult choices. This time, he has to put one of his own agents up as bait for a twisted killer. He knows that Rachel's past has left her broken on the inside, but he has to use her on this case. If they don't stop the killer out there, too many innocent lives will be lost.

"Jack"—The infamous killer known as Jack always leaves a playing card at the scene of his crimes. Only one person has ever survived one of Jack's attacks—and that person is Rachel Mancini. Now Jack is back to make certain that Rachel will not escape him again. Rachel is his—in life and in death.

Prologue

"You should've walked away and dropped the charges. Hell, you should've just given the case to someone else to prosecute. To *anyone* else." Sadness coated his words.

So did fury.

Rachel Mancini jerked against the ropes that held her. Terror clawed through her body. He'd tied her to the chair, secured her so completely.

After he'd drugged her.

The drugs were still in her system. They made her limbs feel sluggish, but the drugs did nothing to numb the terror coursing through her body.

"You should have listened!"

She blinked and found him right in front of her. Adam Wright. The man she'd been dating for the past three months. The man she'd fallen for so easily. He was charming. He was handsome.

He was also a killer.

His hand lifted and she tensed, expecting him to hit her. Instead, his fingers skimmed lightly over her cheek. It was a familiar caress. He'd touched her that way dozens of times. This time his touch seemed to burn her.

"I didn't count on you, Rachel," Adam said, his voice

dropping to a low growl. "The kills are always so easy. I do the work. I get the cash."

This couldn't be happening to her. She and Adam were supposed to go away this weekend. Their first vacation as a couple.

She'd just finished prosecuting her latest case earlier that day. Rachel was a Marine Corps Judge Advocate, and she'd been working on the biggest case of her career. Private First Class Quincy Langam had been accused of murdering two senior officers. Rachel was sure the man was guilty, and she'd done everything possible to give justice to Langam's victims.

Adam's hand dropped away from her face. He pulled out the gun that had been holstered at his hip. "I was paid to kill you."

Her hands twisted against the ropes. Her wrists were bleeding. The flesh had cut quickly against the thick, hemp rope. Rachel ignored the pain. Maybe the blood would help her to slip free of the binds. "I thought you cared about me." All of those months. The flowers. The dates. The laughter and the talking that had gone late into the night. *Everything* had been a lie?

"I don't care about anything." His words were cold now, hollow. The emotion that had blazed in his voice and eyes just moments before was gone.

Adam lifted the gun and aimed it at her.

"Please!" The cry broke from Rachel. This was the man who'd kissed her? Who'd talked to her about a future, a new life? They were supposed to build a life together. "Don't do this, Adam!"

"It's your fault." His jaw hardened. "You should've let someone else handle the case. I could've killed that prosecutor, and you'd be free."

She latched on to what he'd said as she realized just who had sent Adam after her. "Quincy? Quincy Langam hired you?" *Keep him talking.* If Adam was talking, then he wasn't shooting her.

He nodded and didn't lower the gun. He also didn't shoot her. "Quincy's family has a lot of money. Money can hide so much."

"Like the fact that Quincy is a cold-blooded killer?"

Adam smiled at her. "No, he's not cold-blooded. He attacked in the heat of the moment. One of those passion kills. He found his girlfriend with another man, and he erupted. He killed them both. The fact that they were senior officers never mattered to him—it was all personal." Adam gave a little shrug. "All passion, like I said."

Was the rope starting to give around her left wrist? It was! And with another yank, Rachel thought she might be able to slip out of the rope that twisted around her right wrist, too.

"I'm the cold-blooded one," he told her, "and I'm sorry, sweetheart, but you're dead."

No. *No!* Her wrists slipped free of the binds, and Rachel didn't waste any more time begging for her life. She leaped out of that chair, attacking him with all her might.

They collided. Hit the floor. The gun slid from his fingers. She tried to lift her elbow and ram it into him—

But the drugs still had her muscles trembling and weak.

Adam caught her hand easily and he yanked her arm back down. He rolled them on the floor, locking her body beneath his. His green eyes gleamed down at her. "Such a fighter." He yanked her hands above her head and pinned them to the floor. "Some don't fight. They just sit there, crying, as they wait for me to kill them." He flashed the wide smile that used to make her heart skip a beat. "That's just one of the things I love about you."

He *dared* to speak about love even as he prepared to kill her? Rachel slammed her forehead into his nose. She heard the crunch and knew she'd broken cartilage. The sound gave her a savage satisfaction. "You know nothing about love."

He swore at the pain, and his hold weakened. Rachel was a marine, first and foremost, and she was not about to be easy prey. She twisted beneath him, struggling desperately, and she escaped from him as she heaved across the floor.

The gun. She had to get the gun that he'd dropped.

"Yes, I do know about love…."

His voice was so soft she barely heard it.

Rachel grabbed the gun. Her bloody fingers made holding the weapon hard.

Before she could spin toward him with her weapon, Rachel felt the tip of a knife press into her back.

"Do you think…" Adam asked her, seemingly curious "…that you could really do it? Do you think you could kill me?"

Her heart was about to burst out of her chest.

He leaned closer to her. That knife pressed a little deeper into her back. "Because I don't think you can, Rachel. I think that I got to you. The controlled, all-business prosecutor. The brave soldier. I got beneath your skin, and I don't think you've got it in you to actually kill me."

She spun, ignoring the burn of the knife as it sliced over her skin. Rachel brought the gun up and aimed it right at him. "Get away from me," Rachel ordered. Because she would pull that trigger. She *would*.

He dropped the knife, eased back. "I marked you."

Her back throbbed, and she could feel the wetness of her blood soaking her shirt. "And if you come at me again," Rachel told him, "I'll kill you."

He laughed. Adam didn't seem to care that blood was coming from his nose or that she had a gun aimed dead-center at his heart.

"Get your hands up!" Rachel shouted.

He slowly lifted his hands. "A fighter," he whispered again, and he sounded pleased. "But I guess you had to be, right, Rachel? Once a marine, always a marine.... A core of steel hidden beneath the silk."

She stiffened. "Who are you?"

He shrugged his shoulders. "I've got quite a few names...."

She was in a nightmare.

"Most folks just call me Jack," he said, as his eyes narrowed on her. His fingers slid into the pocket of his jeans.

"What are you doing? *Stop!*"

But he didn't pull out a weapon. He pulled out what looked like...a playing card? He tossed it toward her. The card landed at her feet.

The Jack of Hearts.

Her fingers were trembling. That card... Two cards just like that one had recently been found at the scene of two murders in the area. One of the dead had been a witness in the Langam murder case. The other had been Quincy Langam's ex-roommate.

"I'm surprised you're able to stand now," he continued as he rubbed a hand over the line of his jaw. "I hit you with enough sedatives to keep you out for a while. I'd thought about even killing you while you were unconscious…" He hesitated then shook his head. "But that just didn't seem right."

"You're insane." She needed a phone. She had to call the police and get *help*.

"No." Anger flared in his eyes, turning his gaze into green fire. "I'm the man you need to fear."

Her gaze darted around the room. Where were they? The place—it looked like some kind of old, abandoned factory. The room was huge, cavernous, and she was *terrified*.

But a marine didn't let terror stop her. She just kept marching forward.

"What are you going to do?" Adam asked her. "Shoot me?"

"I'm going to call the authorities. You're not going to hurt anyone else."

His eyelids flickered. "So noble. Trying to do the right thing, but you should know…no prison will ever hold me. If the cops come blazing in, then I'll escape, and I'll come back for you."

The words were chilling in their certainty.

"You're mine," he told her. His hands lowered to his sides. "Either mine to kill or mine to love. The choice is all on me… I knew it from the beginning."

"Put your hands back *up!*" Rachel yelled.

He didn't. He took a step toward her.

"Stop!"

"You can't do it," he said, his expression certain. "I know you can't. Because I got to you. I made you feel, didn't I, sweetheart?"

He'd lied to her. Used her. Drugged her. "I can. I will." Her finger tightened on the trigger.

"It's not loaded," he said.

Rachel paused. Her gaze darted down to the gun.

And in that instant, he bent down and yanked a second weapon from his ankle holster.

"No!" Rachel's shout seemed to echo in that huge room.

He fired at her.

She shot back at him.

Rachel fell, hitting the floor. She held on to her gun. She hurt. *Hurt.*

"Such a fighter…" His whisper drifted to her. "All the way to the end."

Rachel tried to bring her gun up.

Then she heard his footsteps, running away.

"Adam?"

He didn't answer.

She didn't let go of the weapon. Rachel tried to pull herself up. The bullet had sunk into her left shoulder. Blood dripped down her arm.

There was no sign of Adam. No, there was no sign of *Jack.*

She stood on her feet, body trembling, wondering if she would be able to chase after him.

But then Rachel heard the pounding thud of footsteps. A lot of footsteps. And that thundering sound was coming toward her.

She turned, aiming her weapon even as the door on the right flew open. Men swarmed inside, men wearing all black and armed with guns of their own.

"Rachel Mancini?" One of the men barked.

Her gaze flew up to his face. He had the darkest eyes she'd ever seen. And the lines of his face looked so hard. So dangerous. Deadly.

"Wh-who are you?" She didn't lower her weapon. So

what if a dozen guns were trained on her right then? The weapon was the only thing she had.

"She's hurt." These terse words came from another man. An older man who stormed into the room with an unmistakable air of command surrounding him. "Get a medic in here now." He pushed through the guns. Headed toward her and acted as if she didn't have a weapon locked on him. "Ms. Mancini, I'm here to help you." His gaze slid around the room. "But first you have to tell me…where is he? Where's Adam Wright?"

Rachel felt a tear leak down her cheek. She never cried. *Never.*

But her entire world had just changed. *I changed.* "I shot him," she heard herself whisper. "But he ran away."

The commander, a man with gleaming eyes, gave a hard nod. He turned back, speaking to the others as he said, "Get a search out now. I want every inch of this building checked."

The team broke up, rushed out.

Except for the commander—and for the man who'd first pointed his weapon at her. The man who'd known her name. His voice had been hard, rumbling, devoid of any accent.

That man came toward her now.

Rachel tensed.

"Easy." His voice was softer than it had been before. "I've got medical training. I can help you." He holstered his weapon and advanced on her.

Her world was falling apart. Rachel wasn't sure that anyone could help her then. She gave a short, negative shake of her head.

Her knees buckled then, and Rachel knew she'd hit the floor soon.

But *he* caught her. The man with the dark eyes. His hands were strong, callused at the fingertips, but he held her gently.

"Who are you?" Rachel asked him again. The world was spinning and that man—the stranger with the dark eyes—was the only thing that seemed solid in that instant.

"Dylan," he told her, his voice a bare rasp of sound.

Over his shoulder, she saw the commander frown at him.

"I'm going to take care of you," Dylan promised her. "We're the good guys. We're going to keep you safe." A pause. "I'm going to keep you safe."

But Rachel didn't believe him. Adam had just taught her the danger of trusting a man. "He's going to come back." She swallowed the lump in her throat. "And he's going to kill me."

Dylan's face hardened. "I won't let that happen."

She still had the gun. Rachel gave him her weapon, but Dylan immediately passed it to the commander. Then she was in Dylan's arms. He carried her out of that room. Carried her out of what was, indeed, an old, abandoned factory.

When the ambulance arrived, Dylan was still there, right at her side.

But no one had found Adam. He'd escaped. Vanished into the night.

I'll come back for you.

Chill bumps rose on Rachel's arms. She knew that, sooner or later, she would be seeing Adam again.

Chapter One

Three years later...

As a rule, the EOD didn't usually handle routine murder investigations.

The EOD—the Elite Operations Division—was an off-the-books covert unit that Uncle Sam liked to pretend didn't exactly exist. The men and women in the EOD were all ex-military. They were lethal, well-trained agents who specialized in hostage rescue and unconventional warfare.

A murder in D.C. shouldn't necessarily catch their attention.

But this was no ordinary murder. And it was far from a routine case.

Dylan Foxx slipped past the cops who waited in the hallway of the high-rise hotel, a hotel that was situated just a few blocks away from Pennsylvania Avenue. They were on the top floor of the hotel, and the cops had all gathered around suite 706. Dylan's boss, Bruce Mercer, had made sure he'd get access to this room. Bruce Mercer controlled most of D.C. from behind the scenes. A puppet master, always pulling the strings.

Dylan entered the room and surveyed the area. The

murder victim lay sprawled near the bed. His blood had pooled and darkened the lush carpet.

One shot to the heart.

Dylan recognized the victim. Hank J. Patterson. Patterson had been a military judge, one of the most respected on the bench.

Patterson spent over fifteen years as an active soldier, but the man hadn't been able to fight back against his attacker. He lay there, no signs of defensive wounds on him, as the scent of death deepened in the suite.

Dylan heard a sharply indrawn breath behind him, and he turned to see Rachel Mancini staring down at the body. Her blue eyes were wide with horror.

He immediately moved to try and block her view. "What are you doing here?" Dylan demanded as fury and fear twisted within him. Because in Patterson's blood, Dylan had seen something—something that triggered a long-held rage within him.

Rachel blinked in surprise. Her hair, a dark curtain of silk, brushed against her jaw as she gave a little shake of her head. "I'm following orders. Mercer called and told me to get down here." She straightened her shoulders. "I'm your teammate, remember?"

As if he could forget. When it came to Rachel, there was never any forgetting for him.

"Where you go," she added, her gorgeous eyes meeting his, "I follow."

But he didn't want her following him into this mess. Rachel could handle danger, he got that, it was just— *I don't want her here. Not on this case. I need her to be safe.*

"That's Hank Patterson," she said, nodding. "I worked with him back when I was a Judge Advocate."

Before Rachel had traded her courtroom days for a life of secrecy with the EOD.

"I've seen plenty of bodies before—you know that," Rachel told Dylan, arching one dark brow. "So just drop the protective routine, okay? Let's get to work."

That was one of his problems. When it came to Rachel, all of his protective instincts went into overdrive. Actually, *most* of his primal instincts did. There was just something about her...

Dylan didn't move. His gaze swept over Rachel's face. Glass-sharp cheekbones, golden skin, full, plump lips. And her eyes—they could bring a man to his knees.

Beautiful. He'd thought that from the first moment he saw her—even though she'd been terrified at the time. Terrified, but still so brave as she held that gun in her shaking grip.

Rachel was one of the strongest women he'd ever met.

Dylan's boss at the EOD agreed with that assessment, which was why the guy had brought Rachel into the fold.

But while Mercer only saw her strength, lately, Dylan was seeing more of Rachel's vulnerability. She could be hurt so easily. Just as she'd been hurt a few months before when one of the EOD's own agents had turned against them.

Rachel had wound up in the hospital and Dylan—for a few minutes there, he'd lost control. When he'd thought Rachel might die, he'd spiraled into a pit of fear that had left him feeling—

"Dylan?" Rachel's voice was soft. Worried. "What's happening?" Her hand lifted and touched his arm.

As always, her touch sent an electric shock right through his system.

"Mercer..." His voice came out too gravelly, so Dylan

tried again, saying, "Mercer didn't tell you why we were being called in?"

"Patterson is military," she said, bringing her body even closer to his. Her scent—the sweet scent reminded him of roses—wrapped around him. "I figured he wanted us to take lead because of—"

"Hank Patterson was executed," Dylan said, breaking through her words. Of course, leave it to Mercer to force this reveal on Dylan. The next bit of news he had to share would wreck Rachel's world, he knew it would. And he hated that he had to put her through more pain.

After a brutal attack by a rogue agent, Rachel had only just been cleared to return to work. She'd left one nightmare, and now she was walking straight into another one.

If he had his way, he'd protect Rachel from anything and everything out there—and from one twisted man in particular.

Still frowning at Dylan, Rachel slipped past him. He noticed that she was careful not to touch anything in the suite. After her time prosecuting, Rachel knew better than to contaminate a crime scene.

She knelt next to the body. Her gaze swept over Patterson. Dylan easily read the sorrow on her face. Then her attention locked on Patterson's wound.

On the blood near him. On what was *in* that blood.

"That's a playing card," Rachel said. Her words shook. Her golden skin had just turned pale. Her head tilted so that she could look up at him, and her eyes were wild with emotion. "Tell me, *tell me that it's not him!*"

Because the EOD was well acquainted with one particular assassin who always left a playing card behind. *Jack.*

Rachel, in particular, was intimately acquainted with the man.

Dylan had gloves on his hands and, carefully, using tweezers, he bent and turned over the playing card so that both he and Rachel could see the face.

The Jack of Hearts stared back up at him.

Rachel surged to her feet. *"No."* Her denial was immediate.

He'd expected that denial.

Dylan turned to the tech who waited silently just a few feet away. He passed the card to the tech. It was bagged and tagged immediately. That evidence would be going back to the EOD for analysis.

As for Rachel...

She hurried from the room.

Dylan didn't follow her, not yet. He stared down at the body then he let his gaze sweep the suite once more. There had been no evidence of a break-in. But that was the way Jack worked. In and out. Fast kills.

And a calling card left behind. The guy always left his card because he liked to claim his kills.

Dylan stayed a few more minutes, needing to be thorough. Crime-scene analysis sure wasn't his area of expertise, but killing— Well, he'd learned plenty about that during his time as a Navy SEAL and as an EOD agent.

He knew he was looking at the work of a professional killer. The man had used a silencer because no one at the hotel had reported hearing a shot. The maid had received a horrifying surprise when she bustled inside to clean the place that morning.

After giving orders to the tech, Dylan exited the room. He wasn't particularly surprised to see Rachel pacing in the hotel's hallway.

When she'd rushed out, he knew that she wouldn't have gone far. That wasn't Rachel's way.

But they didn't speak until they were in the privacy of the elevator. The doors slid closed and Rachel—

"Why didn't you tell me?"

Pain thickened her voice.

He *hated* for Rachel to be in pain. His fist struck out, and he hit the button that would stop the elevator. Immediately, they jerked to a halt.

"If you thought he might be back in D.C....*why didn't you tell me?*" she demanded again.

Dylan turned toward her. Rachel's eyes were so wide—*she'll bring me to my knees.* He locked his jaw and knew he had to stay in control. "I didn't know he was hunting here again. Patterson's death—this is the first time any kill in D.C. has been linked to Jack in three years."

Three long years.

But now that Dylan did know Jack was back...his first instinct was to get Rachel the hell out of that city. He wanted her transferred to someplace safe and sunny while he hunted the maniac known as Jack.

Because Jack will go after her.

"It's not him, is it?" Rachel asked as she rubbed her arms. "It has to be a copycat, right? I mean, three years ago, his exploits were all over the news. Everyone knows about him now."

Jack. The man wasn't a serial killer, at least not in the strict sense of the word. He was an assassin. One who killed for cash.

He was a man with far too much skill when it came to death.

"Tell me that he's a copycat," Rachel said.

He wished he could. Dylan took a step closer to her. He wanted to pull Rachel into his arms and hold her, but that wasn't protocol. He was the team leader. They worked together, side by side. They fought together.

Their relationship was supposed to be professional.

To him, it was so much more.

"Dylan?"

"I can't tell you that. At this point, I don't know who we're dealing with."

"Jack vanished three years ago. After—" Her lips clamped shut, and Rachel didn't say any more. But she didn't have to. He knew her past as well as he knew his own.

Jack had been hired to kill Rachel. Quincy Langam had hired the assassin to kill Rachel and two others who'd been associated with Quincy's case. Two of those people on Langam's kill list had wound up with gunshot wounds to the heart.

Only Rachel had survived.

And Jack disappeared.

"We have intel… Mercer has intel that indicates Jack may have been killing in Europe during the past few years." And leaving his trademark calling card behind. "EOD agents were sent over there—"

"I should have been told!" Now spikes of red color stained her cheeks as anger glinted in her eyes.

Dylan didn't touch that one. He'd been the one to tell Mercer that Rachel *shouldn't* know. "They weren't sure. No one saw the killer to confirm his identity."

"I'm the only one who survived Jack's attack. I should've been there. I could've done something!"

Or Jack could have just come for her.

Again, Dylan found himself sliding even closer to her.

"He eluded the EOD agents in Europe, and now…now it looks like he's come home to do his hunting again."

If they truly were dealing with Jack, the local cops wouldn't handle the case. An international killer—sure, maybe the FBI or the CIA would want a piece of this action, but the EOD would be in charge of the investigation.

Because the targets Jack had taken out—the men and women he always hunted—were tied to military cases. Linked to the U.S. Navy, Air Force, the Marines. There was always a military link for Jack.

And besides, the EOD had a personal interest in the case.

They had Rachel.

"Can you handle this?" Dylan asked her. He had to ask the question as the team leader.

"Of course." Her chin notched up. "I survived him before, didn't I?"

The image of her—bloody, afraid—still haunted him in the darkness of the night.

"If he's back, he'll come for me." Rachel spoke these words with certainty.

"Then he'll have to get *through* me," Dylan fired back, unable to hold those words inside any longer.

Her eyes widened.

He put his hands on her. He *had* to touch her. His fingers curled around her slender shoulders. "He isn't going to have the chance to hurt you. I'll stop him. That's why Mercer has me on the case. He knows I'll do anything necessary in order to make sure that Jack doesn't have the chance to get to you again."

"And what am I supposed to do?" Her body brushed

against his. "Hide? Stay in the shadows while you hunt? That's not who I am, Dylan. You know that."

He did. He knew everything about her.

"Mercer sent me here." She gave a slow nod of her head. "He wants me on the case, and I'm going to stay on it. Jack won't get away with this." A brief pause. "If this *is* Jack."

He wanted to pull her flush against him. To kiss her. They'd worked together for three years, and he'd wanted her that entire time.

But he'd played by the rules and kept his hands off her.

Dreamed of her every night.

"They're going to send hotel guards up soon," Rachel murmured. "Maybe even a firefighter or two."

He blinked.

"You can't keep the elevator stopped forever."

And he couldn't toss Rachel over his shoulder and run away with her. No matter how badly he wanted to do just that.

So he stepped back from her. He started the elevator again, and Dylan focused on breathing. Nice and slow. But he had to ask her, "Do you still love him?"

"What?" Her voice rose, breaking a little on the one word.

That break wasn't what he'd wanted to hear. His gaze held hers. "You loved him three years ago."

"He tried to *kill* me."

"I just want to make sure that emotions won't be a problem for you." His hands clenched into fists. "I have to know that I can count on you."

The elevator had reached the lobby. A soft ding filled

the interior then the doors slid open. Rachel brushed past him. He followed her. "Rachel?"

She turned toward him. "I don't feel any emotion but hate for the guy, okay? So don't worry about me. Nothing is going to cloud my judgment on this mission."

Hate was dangerous. So was fury and fear. He'd have to watch her carefully. *But what else is new there?* He seemed to watch her all the time.

And Rachel didn't know. She had no idea that she'd become his obsession.

"I won't worry." *Lie.* When she shifted away from him, Dylan put his hand on her back and steered her toward the hotel's main desk. "We work this one together."

"Just like always," she murmured. But Rachel was tense beneath his touch. Far too tense.

The hotel manager stared at Dylan with nervous eyes. Dylan flashed him an ID. An official-looking piece that labeled him an FBI agent. The ID was just part of a cover provided by the EOD, but the manager would never know that. "I'm going to need access to every bit of security footage that you've got at this hotel." The EOD would be confiscating that footage. Then their techs would review it, moment by moment, as they looked for the killer.

A killer who seemed to be back, hunting once again in the U.S.

His Rachel was still as beautiful as ever.

Her hair was a little longer. She used to wear it just to her chin, but now it skimmed her shoulders. It was still as dark, still looked as silky.

She was a bit thinner, and there was a new delicacy

to her that hadn't been there before. Probably because of the recent attack she'd suffered.

He'd heard that Rachel had been in the hospital. A knife attack. Some crazed fool had attacked Rachel in her own apartment.

He'd been furious at the news. No one else was supposed to kill Rachel.

She was *his*.

The man with the dark hair stood too close to her. He touched her too much. Even then, his fingers were on her back.

Dylan Foxx. He knew the man's name, and he also knew that Foxx was an EOD Agent.

Foxx had ex-military stamped all over him. It wasn't the too-short hair or the go-to-hell glint that he'd caught in the man's eyes. It was obvious in the battle-ready way he walked. In the gaze that kept sweeping across the room. The guy was looking for threats.

I'm right here, but you don't see me.

Probably because he'd borrowed a cop's uniform. The uniform gave him the up-close access that he needed to the hotel. He'd wanted to see who would be called in for this kill. He'd hoped Rachel would get the case.

She had. Now, finally, things could get interesting again.

He followed two other uniforms out of the hotel. He kept his head down as he walked. Not that he expected anyone to recognize him. Not with the changes he'd been through.

Rachel might look the same. *Just a few slight differences.*

He'd altered completely.

And that was why she would never see him coming. Not until it was far too late.

I've kept my promise, Rachel. I've come back for you.

"Is it him?" Bruce Mercer demanded as his hands flattened on his desk.

Dylan hesitated before answering the boss.

"Don't try to sugarcoat this mess," Mercer snapped at him. "Tell me straight…is he back?"

"It's too early to tell for certain. It could be Jack, or it could be a copycat." He knew Rachel hoped they were dealing with a copycat, anyway.

Mercer's eyes narrowed. As the boss of the EOD, Mercer never pulled his punches. "What does Rachel think?"

Just the mention of her name had Dylan tensing. "She's afraid."

Mercer grunted and rose to pace toward the window that overlooked the D.C. skyline. They were in the main EOD building—not that most folks would ever realize the nondescript structure housed the elite group of agents. To just get through the doors of the building required a level of clearance that the majority of people in the city would never possess.

Mercer stared out at the night for a moment then he said, "She's smart to be afraid. If it is him, then he'll try to make contact with her."

Dylan's fingers tightened around the armrests on either side of his leather chair. "She thinks that, too. Rachel said he'd come for her."

Mercer turned toward Dylan. The EOD boss inclined his head. "She's right."

That wasn't what Dylan wanted to hear. "Do you think he knows she's EOD? Is he aware that she's working with us?"

"I think this assassin knows quite a few things," Mercer murmured. "And I think stopping him is our number-one priority." A rough sigh escaped from Mercer. "As far as I'm aware, this man only has one weakness."

Now that news caught Dylan's attention because he hadn't thought the killer had *any* weakness. "I'll exploit it," he said, more than ready to get his hands dirty on this one. That sicko wouldn't get the chance to hurt Rachel ever—

"Rachel Mancini is his weakness."

Dylan's heart raced in his chest. Instinctively, he shook his head. "The man almost killed Rachel three years ago. She barely escaped him, and you actually think she's some kind of weakness for the guy?" Dylan shook his head. "Mercer, you're usually a whole lot better on this than—"

"Do you wonder *why* he didn't kill her?" Mercer cut through his words.

He didn't wonder. He knew. "Because she fought him. She got away. She *shot* him," Dylan gritted out the words.

"From what I can tell, this man has been making his living as a killer for years. He's never let anyone who he has targeted live, until Rachel. She was his prey. He had her tied up for at least two hours, according to our intel. He could've killed her at any point during that time frame." Mercer rolled back his shoulders. "He didn't."

Dylan didn't like to think of Rachel tied up, scared and alone with the killer known as Jack.

"Did you know that I've recently brought a new profiler into the fold here at the EOD?" Mercer asked.

Talk about a change in topic... Dylan's eyes narrowed on the guy.

"I think you met Noelle Evers before," Mercer continued as he rubbed at the back of his neck. "She worked with the FBI, but I...drafted her and convinced Noelle to join our team. It's on a probationary basis for now because she's not like the others here. No military background." His hand fell to his side. "But I think that's an advantage for her. It lets her see things from a different perspective."

He needed to get Mercer back on track. "Sir—"

"It was Dr. Evers who pinpointed Jack's weakness. She saw what I didn't."

"And what was that?" Dylan wanted out of that office. Actually, he wanted to go and check on Rachel. She'd been so shaken, and Rachel didn't usually show her fear.

Except when Jack is involved.

"Dr. Evers realized that Jack *couldn't* kill Rachel."

That was bull. "He shot at her—"

"And only hit her shoulder. Even though he was less than five feet away from her. Odd, isn't it? For a professional killer, I mean. He *should've* been able to make that shot."

Dylan was just damn grateful he hadn't.

"Dr. Evers thinks that Jack only fired to stop her from hurting him." Mercer's gaze held Dylan's. "The assassin's plan was to get close to Rachel then to kill her. He got close..."

But never killed her.

"A weakness," Mercer repeated. "One that we will use."

Dylan jumped to his feet. "*No*. There is no way I am putting Rachel at risk!" He was protecting her at all costs. "She just got out of the hospital, and you want to send her right into harm's way? *No*. That can't happen."

"I want you with her, Agent Foxx." Mercer's voice had hardened. "Whether we *use* her or not, the fact remains that the man known as Jack could be in D.C. right now, and if he is…you can bet he'll be getting close to Rachel very, very soon."

"When he does, he'll find me in his path." Because *that* was Dylan's plan. Not to use Rachel, not to jeopardize her in any way. But to be there for her. Always.

"That's what I'm counting on," Mercer said, sounding satisfied. He even smiled.

Mercer smiling was a scary sight.

"Go find Agent Mancini. I'll brief you both when I have more information on the Patterson murder."

Dismissed. Fine. Dylan figured it was about time he got away from Mercer. He spun for the door.

"Oh, Agent Foxx?"

He glanced over his shoulder.

"Just be careful," Mercer warned him. The lines near Mercer's eyes deepened. "You don't want Jack's weakness to become your own."

Dylan didn't respond because he already knew that message had come too late.

Rachel had gotten beneath his skin, and, in order to keep her safe, he'd do just about anything.

NORMALLY, RACHEL MANCINI didn't care much for bar scenes. She didn't like the smooth lines that men spouted there so easily. She wasn't comfortable with the flirtatious talk that she was supposed to use in return to their overtures.

As a rule, Rachel had a very hard time trusting men. *Thanks, Adam—or Jack or whoever you really are.*

When the guy you loved tried to kill you, well, it could sure make a girl hesitate when it came to men and future relationships.

But this night wasn't a normal night, and if Rachel hadn't escaped the too-quiet atmosphere of her apartment, she was pretty sure she would have gone crazy.

So she'd fled her apartment and headed down to the corner bar. Actually, the place was more of a pub. O'Sullivan's. Patrick O'Sullivan had opened the pub over twenty years ago, and the place was still thriving in D.C.

The pub was certainly packed that night.

Rachel eased up near the bar. The blond man on her right immediately turned toward her, a wide grin on his face. "Hey there, doll."

Doll? Did she look like a doll?

Tall, tan and with carefully tousled blond hair, the guy beside her could have stepped right off the set of some cologne commercial. His smile broadened as he stared at her. His blue gaze swept over her body, way too slowly, before finally returning to her face. "A girl like you shouldn't be alone tonight."

"But that's exactly what I want to be," she murmured back and she semi-tried to keep the annoyed edge out of her voice.

A frown creased the blond's brow.

But the bartender, obviously having overheard her, laughed.

She glanced his way. The bartender, a dark-haired guy

with a well-trimmed beard that covered his jaw, offered her a grin. "What can I get you?" He leaned toward her. "Want to start with Paddy's Whiskey?"

That sounded like a fine plan to her. Rachel nodded.

He winked. "Be right back." The faint hint of Ireland rolled beneath his words. He was a good-looking guy. Nice features. Light blue eyes.

So why did she look at the bartender and find herself thinking about a man who didn't look quite so handsome...a man who always appeared a bit dangerous? A man with dark eyes—eyes that she swore could see straight through her.

Dylan Foxx.

Her gaze shifted away from the bartender.

"You don't *have* to be alone," the blond next to her said. Obviously, her earlier comment had gone right over his head.

She gave him a smile. Polite, but firm, Rachel said, "That's the way I want to be tonight."

Unfortunately, that was also the way she was every night.

Three years had passed, but Rachel still tensed at the thought of any man slipping past her defenses. Any man except—

"You heard the lady." That low, growling voice came from behind her. And she knew only one man with a voice like that—Dylan. "Looks like you're striking out here, buddy. So go try your luck someplace else."

The blond glared at him. Rachel turned, shaking her head as she gazed up at Dylan. "What are you doing here?" Sure, Dylan wasn't like her. He visited plenty of bars. But he lived across town.

And this bar was practically in her backyard.

"I came looking for you."

His words had her tensing. "Has something happened? Has—"

She broke off, realizing that Dylan wasn't actually looking at her. He was too busy glaring back at the blond. The guy was just sitting there, staring at them.

"Leave," Dylan barked, using the voice that sent even seasoned EOD agents fleeing. "Now."

The blond guy fled, but he muttered, "Should've said she had a boyfriend..." as he stormed away.

Dylan immediately took the guy's seat. He exhaled as he got comfortable. "Better. Much better."

The bartender appeared with her drink. He slid it across the table toward Rachel. "On the house," he said with a wink.

Surprised, Rachel found herself smiling back at him. "Thank you."

"It's the least I can do for a neighbor." Again, that Irish whispered in his voice. "You don't know me, but I've heard plenty about you."

His words surprised her.

"My grandfather, Patrick, told me to keep a look out for you, Rachel Mancini."

She knew Patrick. When she'd first moved into the city, Patrick had been the first person she'd met.

But he'd passed away a few months ago. "I'm so sorry about your grandfather—"

The bartender held up his hand. "So am I, but he

wouldn't want us grieving. To him, life was for celebrating."

Yes, that was the way Patrick had thought of life—just that way. She'd never seen him without a smile on his face.

"My name's Aidan. Aidan O'Sullivan. And it's good to finally meet you." He offered his hand to her.

Rachel shook that hand, and quickly let him go. For some reason, she was far too conscious of Dylan's stare on her.

Aidan glanced at Dylan. "What can I get for you?"

"Whiskey."

Her gaze darted toward him. *He's still watching me.*

"I have everything else that I need," Dylan said.

He didn't mean those words the way they sounded. Rachel was sure of that.

Aidan laughed and got the drink. "Hope you have better luck than the last one." He pushed the whiskey toward Dylan.

Dylan's fingers curled around the glass. "I will."

Rachel took a quick gulp of her drink. It burned, in a good way, as it slid down her throat.

Dylan emptied his whole glass in one swallow. His eyes stayed on hers. He had the deepest, darkest eyes she'd ever seen. So dark they almost looked black.

His hair was black and thick. It was cut short and the cut just accentuated the hard lines of his face. Dylan wasn't technically handsome. Rachel had to remind herself of that fact every few days. He wasn't, though. He was more...dangerous. Rough. His jaw was square and firm, his cheeks were sharp angles, and Rachel was pretty sure that he'd broken his nose a time or two in bar fights over the years.

Dylan Foxx was an ex-Navy SEAL. As far as she knew, the guy feared absolutely nothing in the world. He was her team leader at the EOD. He was the man who had her back on every mission. The one man she trusted above all others.

He was also the man who was off-limits to her.

Actually, as far as Rachel was concerned, all men were off-limits. She'd made a near-fatal mistake with the last man she'd let get too close.

She wasn't planning on getting burned—or *attacked*— again.

Rachel cleared her throat. "How did you know I was here?" Because Rachel knew it wasn't some coincidence that he was in the pub, too.

He leaned toward her. Whenever he got too close, Rachel had the feeling that Dylan surrounded her. Maybe it was because of his shoulders. His shoulders were so wide. Muscled. Or maybe it was just because of...*Dylan.*

The guy seemed to dominate everything and everyone around him.

"I was on my way to your place," he told her, voice low. "Then I saw you heading in here."

She took another quick gulp of her drink. Perhaps she should be sipping it, but Rachel was too tense for that. "Why were you coming to my place?" Rachel pushed.

His eyelids flickered. "Because I wanted you."

No, he had *not* just said that. The pub was too loud. She'd misheard him. "Wh-what?"

A furrow appeared between his dark brows as he leaned even closer to her. His crisp, masculine scent teased her nose. "Because I wanted to talk with you."

Right. That made more sense. Her too-eager imagination had twisted his words.

"But this isn't the place to talk." He tossed some cash onto the bar, and his hand wrapped around hers. "Come on, let's go."

She should say that she'd just gotten there. That she wasn't ready to leave.

But I am. She didn't want to dodge pick-up lines and leering guys. Rachel had come to the bar because she couldn't stand the silence.

There would be no silence with Dylan.

She rose.

His fingers twined with hers.

Rachel glanced down at their hands. That was new. He'd never *held* her hand before. Sure, Dylan seemed to touch her pretty frequently. He'd brush back her hair or he'd squeeze her shoulders, but never something quite so intimate as actually holding her hand.

"Dylan?" Her voice was so soft that she wasn't even sure he'd heard her.

He didn't respond, but he did lead her through the crowd, pulling her toward the door. Bodies brushed against her, making Rachel tense, then they were outside. The night air was crisp, and taxis rushed by them on the busy street.

Dylan still held her hand.

He turned and pulled her toward the side of the brick building. Then he caged her with his body. "Want to tell me what you were doing?" An edge of anger had entered his words.

Rachel blinked at him. "Uh, getting a drink?" That part had seemed pretty obvious.

"What you were doing with the blond, Rachel? The blond jerk who was leaning way too close to you in that pub."

The same way that Dylan had been leaning close?

"Now isn't the time for you to start looking for a new guy." *Definite* anger now. "We need to find out if Jack is back here, killing. We don't need you to hook up with some—"

She shoved against his chest.

The move caught them both off guard.

Beneath the streetlamp, Rachel saw Dylan's eyes widen.

"You don't get to control my personal life," Rachel told him flatly. *What personal life?* The fact that she didn't have one wasn't the point. "And neither does Jack. Got it?"

He gazed back at her.

"On missions, I follow your orders. But what I do on my own time…that's *my* business." She stalked away from him, heading back toward her apartment building.

Then she heard the distinct thud of his footsteps as Dylan rushed after her. *He'd better be coming to apologize.*

Right. She'd never actually heard Dylan apologize for anything.

His fingers curled around her arm. He spun her back to face him. "Your last lover was a killer. I'd think that you'd want to—"

"You're wrong!" The words erupted from her.

And something strange happened to Dylan's face. They were right under the streetlight, so it was incredibly easy for her to read his expression. Surprise flashed first, slackening his mouth, but then fury swept over his face. A hard mask of what truly looked like rage. *"You're involved with someone else? You're sleeping with someone?"*

Since when did she have to check in with Dylan about her love life? "He wasn't my lover."

His hold tightened on her. "What?"

"Adam. Jack. Whatever he's calling himself. He. Wasn't. My. Lover." There. She'd said it. It felt good to get that out. "We were going away together that weekend. We hadn't..." Rachel cleared her throat. "He wasn't my lover." She yanked away from him, angry now, too. "Not that it's any of your business who I'm sleeping with—"

"It is." He snarled the words and he yanked her up against his chest. "It shouldn't be...but it is."

And his mouth took hers.

Chapter Two

He shouldn't have kissed her. Dylan knew that truth all the way down to his soul. His hands were supposed to stay off her.

But instead, he was pulling her as close as he could get her.

He'd fantasized about her mouth too many times. Red, bow-shaped lips. That plump lower lip. He'd wanted her mouth on his. Wanted her.

Now he had her.

Her taste made him drunk. It gave him a far better rush than the whiskey. Her breasts were pressed against his chest. His hips pushed against her.

And the woman had to be feeling just how turned on he was by her. When Rachel walked into a room, hell, he got turned on instantly. There was no stopping his reaction to her.

She didn't shove him away again. He expected her to push him back, but she didn't. Her mouth opened slightly and her tongue slipped out to rub lightly against his own.

Every muscle in his body tensed.

Rachel.

His hold hardened on her. He licked her lips then took the kiss deeper, sampling her, savoring her. His heartbeat thudded in his ears. The thunder of that beat drowned out the sound of traffic on the nearby street.

She was the only thing he felt.

The only thing he wanted.

His fingers slid down her back, curved over her hips and brought her even closer to him. He didn't want any barriers between them. He wanted her as wild for him as she was in his dreams.

His.

A soft moan slipped from her lips, and he drank it up, greedy for more. He wanted everything she had to give. He'd *take* everything.

But not there. Not on the street. Not with all of the eyes and ears that could be on them.

And with Jack out there, waiting to strike?

His mouth lifted from hers. He stared down at Rachel, watching as her eyes slowly opened. She blinked up at him.

She was the most beautiful woman he'd ever seen.

What have I done?

He forced his hands to free her, when he wanted to hold as tightly to her as possible. "I should apologize," Dylan began.

She pushed back her hair. The dark mane that he wanted to see spread out on his pillow.

"I should," he continued, voice rough with desire, "but I'm not."

Her breath seemed to come in fast pants. She wasn't the only one breathing too hard. Dylan felt as if each breath he took sawed out of his lungs.

"We're not on duty," he said. "And I've been wanting to taste you for too long."

Rachel backed away from him. "You can't do this

now. You *can't.*" She spun on her heel and started marching down the street. Her steps were fast and hard.

Dylan followed right behind her, but his pace was much slower as he tailed Rachel back to her apartment building.

Rachel's apartment was on the second floor, and she hit the stairs leading up to that level at a near run. Dylan lifted a brow at her haste, and then he headed up after her, taking his time.

At the top of the stairs, he turned to the left. Rachel's apartment was the one on the end. The one that gave her a perfect view of the rising sun. Not that he'd ever been there to watch the sun rise with Rachel...

Maybe one day.

Rachel unlocked her apartment. The security alarm began to beep. Dylan followed her inside and shut the door as she reset the alarm. He propped his back up against the wooden door frame and waited for her to erupt.

In his experience, Rachel liked to do her eruptions in private. She wasn't the public drama type.

Only she didn't erupt. She wrapped her hands around her waist, and she stared up at him.

Rachel appeared...lost. Afraid. Of him?

The look in her eyes actually hurt him. He jerked away from the door. "Rachel—"

"I don't expect an apology," she said and the words came out too quickly. "Especially since I was kissing you back."

Yes, she had been. And she'd just been adding more fuel to his fantasies.

"But...*why?*" Her question was stark. "Why now?"

Because jealousy had clawed into him when he'd

thought that Rachel might be involved with someone else. He'd been at her side, working day and night with her for three years. He'd wanted her that whole time.

He'd never thought another man might take her away from him…

Until tonight.

When he'd walked in that pub and seen the blond eyeing Rachel like she was the best candy he'd ever seen, Dylan realized that Rachel could slip right through his fingers. Fear had grown with him. Then, outside, when he'd confronted Rachel on the street—

You're involved with someone else? You're sleeping with someone? His own furious words seemed to blast back at him.

And, deep inside, Dylan wondered just what he would have done if Rachel had been involved with another man.

"Rachel…"

Her rough laughter cut him off. Rachel didn't laugh often. In fact, he had to fight in order to get her to ever lower her guard enough to laugh just a little with him. When she did laugh, the sound was light. Soft. As beautiful as she was. Not mocking and cold.

"Mercer," she said, giving a hard nod of her head as if she'd just figured out a challenging puzzle. "You went to see him tonight, didn't you? Before you came to look for me."

On full alert now, Dylan nodded.

She spun, giving him her back as she paced toward her couch. "I should have known."

Now he was lost. "Known what?"

She turned back to glare at him. "I've worked enough missions with Mercer to know how his mind works. I know his plays. All of his little mind games." She waved her hand in the air. A rough gesture as her fingers spun in a little circle. "He thinks he's going to use me, doesn't he?"

That was far too close to Mercer's plan, so Dylan didn't speak. He did advance toward her, moving cautiously.

"But it's not just Mercer." Her head cocked as she studied Dylan. "It's you, too, isn't it?"

He froze. "Using you isn't on my agenda."

"No?" Again, her laughter seemed to mock him—and herself. "I'm the only person to survive one of Jack's attacks. If he's back in D.C., then we all know he'll be gunning for me."

Mercer thought there was a whole lot more involved than just the guy's desire to end some unfinished killing business.

Dylan didn't know what was happening yet.

"I was the guy's girlfriend. So you and Mercer got together and you thought—what? That you'd try to stir things up by making it look as if you and I were involved? That way, you'd be able to stay extra close to me so that you could get the drop on Jack."

He planned to stay extra close to her, no matter what.

"Seduction." Her voice became a whisper on that one word, and he had to strain in order to hear her. Then she cleared her throat, and, voice louder, asked, "Mercer's idea? Or yours? I know he's gotten his agents to seduce women in the past." Disgust tightened her features. "He's used the women as bait in his traps, but for you to use me like this—"

He was across the room in two seconds. He reached for her, but Rachel flinched back from him.

When he couldn't touch her, his hands fisted. "It's not like that."

"Oh?" Doubt was there, plain to see on her face. "Mercer doesn't think he can use me?"

He wouldn't lie to her. To Rachel—*not ever.* "He does."

She took a step back. "And you kissing me tonight—"

"Didn't have a damn thing to do with Mercer or Jack. I kissed you because *I* wanted to do it. No other reason." Because in that one instant, the control he usually maintained had cracked. He'd reacted, driven by the primitive impulse to possess her.

Rachel shook her head. Her dark locks slid over her shoulders. "I don't believe you. Three years pass and you never so much as hint that you're interested in me, then we figure out that Jack might be back in town, and all of a sudden you're holding me, kissing me on the street." Her shoulders straightened. "A femme fatale, I'm not. I get that. I just—I didn't think you'd do this to me."

He wasn't doing anything to her.

"I don't need a guard tonight," Rachel continued as her eyes glittered. She had gorgeous eyes. Big, so blue. "I'm in my apartment, safe for the night. So you can leave. Just...*leave.*"

He didn't want to leave.

She headed toward her bedroom. "Lock the door on your way out. You know how to set the security system." Her sigh drifted back to him. "At this point, I guess you know everything about me, don't you?"

No, he didn't. *I didn't know you hadn't slept with Jack.*

She opened her bedroom door and didn't look back. The door closed behind her with a soft squeak.

Dismissed. It didn't get more obvious than that. He turned, preparing to get out, as ordered. Rachel had it all wrong, though. Kissing her sure hadn't been Mercer's plan.

It had been mine.

His hand lifted above the security panel. He would convince Rachel tomorrow. He'd get her to listen to him then and—

"Dylan!" Rachel's scream had him whirling around and racing for her bedroom.

She met him in the doorway, her eyes wide and her body trembling.

He grabbed her and pulled her close. Rachel had faced down enemies in every hot spot on earth, but she was shaking in her own apartment. "What is it?" Dylan asked, looking for a threat.

She licked her lips. "He was here."

He pushed her behind him and rushed into her bedroom. His gaze darted to the left, then to the right.

Then he focused on her bed. The large, four-poster sat in the middle of the room. The bed covers had been turned back. He advanced, eyes narrowing.

On her pillow, someone had carefully positioned a playing card.

The Queen of Hearts.

"This isn't a copycat," Rachel said. She stood in the doorway. "A copycat wouldn't know about me."

Because the EOD had made sure Rachel's identity was kept from the press. No reporters even knew about her attack.

"He wants me to know that he's here." Her words were husky. "And he's coming after me."

"I CAN'T JUST…stay with you," Rachel said as she glanced around Dylan's place. Sure, she'd been in his home plenty of times before.

But he hadn't just *kissed* her before.

"The techs are going over your apartment. They're going to scan that place from top to bottom." He crossed his arms over his chest and leveled a hard stare at her. "You know they'll be there all night. Do you really just want to stay there and watch them? Or do you want to get some sleep so you'll be ready for whatever game Jack plans to play tomorrow?"

Technically, it already *was* tomorrow. A quick glance at Dylan's wall clock showed her it was close to 2:00 a.m., but Rachel didn't feel tired. Too much adrenaline spiked through her blood.

He was in my home. Jack had managed to slip inside her home. He'd gotten right past the security system that was supposed to be state-of-the-art.

"What if he'd been there?" Dylan suddenly demanded.

She rubbed her temples. They were throbbing. Just the mention of Jack made them do that.

"He could've killed you," Dylan continued, voice almost snarling.

She wasn't sure what was happening with Dylan. Normally, the guy was Mr. Controlled. Dylan was the voice of reason on their missions. But he seemed to vibrate with a barely contained intensity, and Rachel had the feeling that he was very close to an explosion.

"We searched the apartment," Rachel reminded him.

"No one was there. His goal tonight wasn't my death. He just wanted me to know he was here."

So now she'd be looking over her shoulder. Wondering if he was close by, watching her.

But she wondered that already. When a man promised to kill you, well, that kind of promise left an impression on a woman.

"He got past your security." Now Dylan was pacing. He did that when he plotted and planned—quick, tight pacing.

"We know he's good. The guy's practically a ghost."

"He's good." Dylan's lips tightened. "I'm better." And he headed toward her.

Rachel couldn't help it, she tensed at his approach.

But all Dylan said was, "Take my bed. I'll bunk down on the couch. In the morning, we'll get a plan going, and we *will* catch this guy."

Oh, right. He hadn't been coming over to kiss her. That had been a one-shot deal. Rachel wet her too-dry lips. For an instant, she could almost taste him. *Stop it. Stay focused.* "I can take the couch." Dylan was six foot three. His legs would dangle over the end of that thing. He should take the king-size bed. She'd be fine on the couch.

"I want you in my bed."

Her heart raced even faster. *Still from the adrenaline.*

His hand lifted, and he brushed back the hair that had fallen over her brow. "It's going to get worse, Rachel. You know it is. Jack won't go down easily. The man's a vicious killer."

And I once thought I was falling in love with him.

"You need rest. Good rest. Not the kind you'll find on my lumpy couch."

They'd watched TV on that couch plenty of times. Horror movies. Baseball games. They'd shared popcorn.

He never kissed me then.

Even though she'd wanted him to do it. She'd wanted his mouth on hers so many times.

"Rachel?" he prompted.

She realized that she was simply standing there, staring up at him. "Ah...you need rest, too. You won't be able to sleep on the couch, either."

His smile came then. She hadn't expected it, and, as always, the sight of that slow, sexy grin made her stomach twist. "Now, Rachel," he murmured, "are you inviting me to share my bed with you?"

Her breath caught. She felt fire sting her cheeks. "Take the couch." Rachel whirled and nearly ran into his bedroom.

His soft laughter followed her.

That laughter...it made her feel safe. But then, Dylan had a way of usually making her feel safe. He had from the very beginning. When she'd looked up in that nightmare, when blood had soaked her, he'd been there.

I'm going to take care of you. And he had. He'd stayed with her in the hospital, then later trained her at the EOD. He'd gone on every mission with her.

Dylan was her best friend. She'd forgive him for following Mercer's orders. A temporary mess-up.

Tomorrow they'd get back to working as a team.

Rachel hurriedly undressed and pulled back the covers. No playing card waited for her this time.

She slid beneath the sheets. They were cool, and the bed smelled of him. Rachel inhaled, drinking in that crisp scent. She pulled the covers up to her chin.

The bed was too big, and Dylan—even though he wasn't in the room—seemed to fill the space.

She closed her eyes and tried to calm her heartbeat.

DYLAN STARED AT the closed bedroom door.

He finally had Rachel in his bed.

Only he wasn't occupying it with her. It figured that would be his luck.

He grabbed some blankets and a spare pillow from his closet then he did his best to bunk down on the couch. Rachel had been right. His legs dangled off the end of that thing.

But comfort wasn't exactly high on his list of priorities. Taking care of Rachel, that ranked right up at the top of his to-do list.

He shoved a fist into the pillow, trying to plump it up. Fury still heated his blood. *The maniac had been in her apartment. In her home.*

Had Jack still been near the scene when Rachel and Dylan returned to her place? Watching from a distance?

What if Rachel had gone home alone? Would Jack have tried to make contact with her?

Not on my watch. The guy would discover that Rachel was much better protected this time around. Jack wouldn't get close to her.

The killer would be captured. Locked up.

And then you won't ever see Rachel again, Jack.

RACHEL HAD A NEW LOVER.

Rage built within Jack as he stared up at the dark building. Rachel had vanished in there with the other EOD agent, Dylan Foxx.

Jack knew all about the EOD. They'd been hunting him for years, so he'd done his best to learn all their secrets.

He knew Rachel had joined them. *Because of me.* Even as he'd fled the U.S., the EOD had recruited her, and his Rachel had only been too eager to join them.

Her first mistake.

And Jack could forgive *one* mistake.

But two? Two mistakes?

Mistake number two is sleeping with Dylan Foxx. Rachel should know better. She'd promised to be his.

A second mistake deserved punishment. Poor Rachel. But she had a lesson to learn.

His hand lifted and his fingers lightly stroked the scar under his T-shirt. Rachel's mark. She'd hit him with her bullet, but just like him, she hadn't aimed for the heart.

Because Rachel knew the truth, just as he did. They were meant to be together. Two halves of a very, very perfect whole. She was the only one who could complete him.

He turned from the building, hunching his shoulders. Dylan Foxx had made a fatal mistake. The man had touched Rachel, kissed her, right there on the street. For all to see.

And I saw.

Until that moment, Jack had thought that the two were just friends. He'd kept such a careful watch on Rachel over the years. A watch she never even realized.

She'd had no lovers. *So I was told.*

But now, things *had* changed for Rachel. That change just wouldn't do. Rachel could only have one lover—*and that lover will be me.*

Dylan Foxx would need to be eliminated.

Hmmm…perhaps his elimination *would* be Rachel's

punishment. When Dylan Foxx died before her, Rachel would realize just what a serious mistake she'd made.

Jack whistled as he headed deeper into the night.

A POUNDING ON his door woke Dylan hours later. He kicked away the covers and, clad only in a pair of jeans, he stomped toward the door. A quick glance out the peephole showed him the identity of his visitor.

Growling in disgust, Dylan yanked open the door. "What do you want?" he demanded.

The man on his threshold just laughed. "Ah, Dylan, always a pleasure, isn't it?"

No, it wasn't. Dylan's eyes narrowed as he studied Thomas "Dragon" Anthony. He and Thomas didn't exactly get along, and a few months back, when Dylan had thought that Thomas might be the rogue agent at the EOD, he'd even…shot the guy.

At the time, though, Dylan had been feeling barely sane. He'd just discovered Rachel, covered in blood, and Thomas had been at the scene. He'd ordered the man to stand down, but—

"Don't worry, man," Thomas said, golden eyes glinting as he seemed to sense Dylan's thoughts. "It was only a flesh wound."

Because Dylan had *chosen* for it to be. "If I'd wanted you dead," Dylan growled right back at him, "you'd be in the ground now."

Thomas stepped forward.

"What's going on?" Rachel called out.

Dylan glanced over his shoulder. Rachel had just slipped from his bedroom. She had on—

She's wearing my shirt. One of his old navy T-shirts.

It seemed to swallow her, falling all the way down to her knees. She looked sexy as hell in that shirt.

She also had a gun in her hand. *His* gun.

"What's happening?" she asked as she crept closer. Her suspicious gaze was on the door. She hadn't seen Thomas yet.

And, lucky for Thomas, he hadn't seen her.

"It's okay," Dylan said, turning toward her and making sure that he put his body in front of hers. Rachel had some truly gorgeous legs. Long, golden. Perfect.

"You should get dressed," he told her, aware that his voice sounded a little too thick. "Then come back out so we can talk."

"I heard voices. I thought you might need me so I grabbed the first thing I saw."

Hmmm…he wondered…had the first thing been the shirt? Or the gun?

She craned her head so she could see over his shoulder. Her eyes widened. *"Thomas?"*

"Looking good, Rachel," Thomas murmured back.

Dylan spun around, a snarl on his lips.

But Rachel laughed. "Well, considering the last time you saw me, I was covered in blood and nearly unconscious on the floor, I guess I do look better."

Dylan didn't like to think about that time. The rogue agent had targeted Rachel. Dylan had been so desperate during those long hours while she'd undergone surgery.

So afraid.

Before Rachel, he hadn't feared anything. She'd changed him, and he wasn't sure that change was for the better.

"You weren't the only bloody one," Thomas told her.

"Your trigger-happy team leader made sure I wasn't a threat."

Dylan glared at him. "I told you to stand down. Maybe next time you'll follow orders."

Rachel's feet padded away from him. The bedroom door closed. Good. She was getting dressed. Thomas wouldn't be able to ogle her legs.

The way I was doing.

"Come on now," Thomas said as he shut the door behind him. "We both know what really happened. You thought I'd hurt Rachel, and you went a little…over the edge."

Dylan felt a muscle jerk in his jaw. "Why are you here?"

Thomas shrugged. "Mercer's afraid you might have another one of those little *over the edge* moments since this particular case is so personal. Since your usual backup—Cooper Marshall—is out of town on his honeymoon, the big boss sent me to keep watch on you and Rachel."

Great. Just what he needed. Thomas already seemed a little *too* interested in Rachel as it was.

Thomas lifted his hands in the air. "Consider me part of your team from here on out."

Not what he wanted. Thomas had a reputation within the EOD. The guy was a martial arts expert, and that expertise had earned him the moniker of Dragon. His particular skill set made him the perfect killing machine—and Thomas had killed plenty of times. His specialty was hand-to-hand combat. He could kill an enemy instantly, and his prey never would have the chance to so much as whisper for help.

Thomas had been captured behind enemy lines a year

ago. By the time Dylan and his team had gotten in to free
the man, Thomas had already killed all of his captors.

And the man hadn't even had a weapon.

But Thomas had been injured. Grievously so. It had
been touch and go on the chopper ride out of that place.
Rachel had stayed with Thomas every moment. She'd
applied pressure to his wounds. She'd kept the man alive,
talking to him, telling him that everything would be
okay.

And Thomas had made it. He'd pulled through.

*Only, now do you have too much of an interest in Ra-
chel?* Dylan sure thought so. "Another agent will probably work better," he said, giving a decisive nod. "I'll talk
with Mercer when we go in to the office today. Thanks,
Dragon, but your services aren't—"

"You know that I owe her." Thomas's cool voice in-
terrupted Dylan's words. "Let me repay the debt."

The bedroom door opened behind them.

Dylan glanced at Rachel. She'd dressed in fresh jeans
and a T-shirt. She'd picked up a small overnight bag
last night, right before he'd hustled her out of her place.
Her dark hair was pulled back in a ponytail. She looked
younger. Vulnerable.

But the truth was that Rachel Mancini really was far
from defenseless *or* delicate. She'd been a marine, then
a Marine Corps Judge Advocate. In the courtroom, she'd
been a powerhouse. Then, when she'd joined the EOD,
Rachel had proven herself time and again. She put her
life on the line. She fought to protect her teammates.

Now they would protect her.

*Sorry, Rachel, for what's coming. But I won't keep
risking you.* He'd created his own plan last night when
he'd tossed and turned on that lumpy couch.

"Thomas is our backup on this mission," Dylan said.

"The mission?" Rachel repeated.

"Apprehending and containing the assassin known as Jack." As Mercer had said, that was priority. He inclined his head toward Thomas. "Welcome to the team." *And if you mess up, if you put her in any jeopardy, you'll answer to me.*

Thomas nodded back to him. Dylan knew that his message had been received. Loud and clear.

Good. The Dragon's reputation didn't scare Dylan. If Thomas did anything to endanger Rachel, Dylan wouldn't stop until he'd destroyed the other man.

JACK STARED THROUGH his scope as the three EOD agents filed out of Dylan Foxx's building.

The scope focused on them, one at a time. The man in front was new—dark hair, tall, muscled. He walked with the same *too-aware* tenseness that Dylan Foxx did. *Ex-military.* At the EOD, they pretty much all were.

That didn't give them an advantage.

I'm ex-military, too. Only they didn't know that because they didn't know anything about him. To the EOD agents, he was a ghost.

Well, he was a ghost to everyone but *her.* Rachel knew him for the flesh-and-blood man that he was.

He focused on Rachel. Her hair was pulled back. He didn't like that. He'd told her time and again to wear her hair down. He preferred it free around her face. She knew he was out there, and she should've worn her hair for him.

The scope stayed on her. But then…then Dylan moved. The guy positioned himself right in front of Rachel.

Jack's back teeth ground together as he leaned in

for the shot. It would be so easy. He could fire right then. The bullet would find its target, and Dylan Foxx wouldn't be a threat any longer.

But Rachel was too close to Dylan.

Jack was a good shot, damn good, but Rachel was so unpredictable. She might lunge at the last moment. She might grab Dylan. Try to shield him.

The bullet could hit her.

No, it was safer to wait. A better moment would come.

Dylan and Rachel climbed into the back of a black SUV. The new agent hurried around to the front and jumped in the driver's side.

The vehicle rushed away.

Jack put down his weapon. *Next time.*

But his gaze tracked to Dylan's building. Hmmm… just what could he learn inside that place?

He put his weapon back in his car. To the rest of the world, it looked as if he were carrying around a guitar case. A little trick he'd learned from one of his favorite movies a long time ago.

He slipped into the building. He'd scoped out this place a time or two before.

He entered Dylan's place through the front door. There was a fire escape, but going that way would just attract too much attention. The alarm began to beep, but a few fast strokes and some quick rewiring of the base pad had shut the system off.

Then he turned and stared at Dylan Foxx's home.

Know your enemy. That was rule number one for him. Whenever he had a new target, Jack made it his mission to learn everything he could about that person.

It was time to learn Dylan Foxx's secrets.

He walked past the couch and glanced around. No family photographs. No mementos. The guy was a soldier, through and through. No, a shadow.

Are you trying to be a ghost, like me?

Jack had on gloves as he quickly searched through Dylan's desk. Again, no photos.

The guy's computer was password protected. Getting past that system shouldn't be a problem, either, but he'd save it for a bit later.

Jack entered the bedroom.

Pillows and what looked like extra blankets were piled onto the bed. And…

He stepped closer to the bed. It was faint, but he caught Rachel's scent in the air. She'd been in the bedroom, in the *bed,* with Dylan Foxx. His breathing came faster as the blood within his veins seemed to boil.

His gaze fell on the wall to the right. Framed, black-and-white photographs filled that wall. The photographs were of D.C. landmarks—the Ford's Theatre, the Lincoln Memorial, the Washington Monument. He stared at those images, caught by a pang of familiarity.

Those were Rachel's work. The angles of the images, the use of light, the stark white-and-black contrast—he'd seen her work before.

She'd given the images to Dylan Foxx, and the man had put them up on his bedroom wall.

The attachment is there. Dylan is more than just a teammate.

Jack stormed toward the nightstand and yanked it open.

And inside…he found a photograph. A framed picture of Rachel. She was smiling. She looked *happy.*

In that picture, she was standing right beside Dylan Foxx. The guy had his arm wrapped around Rachel's shoulders.

Jack's fist slammed into the glass, shattering it.

DYLAN'S PHONE BEGAN to beep. He yanked it up and cursed when he saw the screen. "Turn the vehicle around," he ordered Thomas. "Now."

Thomas braked. The SUV jerked to a stop.

"What's happening?" Rachel asked as she turned toward him.

Dylan looked at her. "I have a few backup security devices at my place. Someone just triggered one of those alarms."

Her eyes widened.

Thomas spun the vehicle around.

Dylan scrolled through the alerts that had just come through on his phone. "The main system is showing an all-clear signal, but the motion sensor in the bedroom says that someone is in there right now."

"Jack?" Rachel whispered.

He thought so. Because Jack was good at getting past security systems. *You just weren't good enough this time.*

The tires squealed as Thomas raced back toward Dylan's building.

JACK STEPPED ON pieces of the shattered frame. Dylan had just revealed too much.

She was in his bed. He keeps her photograph close.

Jack advanced toward the door.

And his gaze lifted, just for a moment. He saw the small white box mounted in the corner of the bedroom, about a foot away from the door. A little, red light glinted on that box.

Motion sensor.

He smiled. Well, well. Jack wondered how much time he'd have before Dylan came racing back to the scene.

Jack bent and pulled the knife from the sheath at his ankle. If Dylan got back too quickly, then Jack would handle him.

Maybe today will be the day that you die, Dylan Foxx. Jack strode out of the bedroom.

As soon as Thomas's SUV stopped at the edge of the sidewalk, Rachel jumped from the vehicle. She ran toward Dylan's building.

Dylan grabbed her arm. His hold hauled her back around. "What are you doing?"

Uh, her job? She had her weapon out, and she was ready to confront Jack.

"We go in together," Dylan said as his hold tightened on her. "We don't know what we might find inside."

Her heartbeat wouldn't slow down. Rachel was usually pretty cool in combat situations. As a marine, she *had* to be cool. Going in too hot or too wild would just be dangerous.

But this wasn't a normal combat situation. This wasn't even a normal mission. This was Jack.

Thomas joined them. He also had his gun out.

It was a good thing Dylan's building was fairly isolated. He was the only one on the second floor. The first floor was empty—and owned by Dylan.

If any neighbors *had* been around, the sight of the weapons would've sent them all fleeing.

"I lead," Dylan said. "Thomas, you stay down here

just in case he tries to run." His gaze held Rachel's. "You watch my back. I watch yours."

That was the way it normally was for them. Rachel nodded.

They rushed up the flight of stairs that would take them to the second level. Her feet pounded in a fast rhythm that nearly matched her heartbeat. They burst onto the second floor.

Dylan's door was shut.

He glanced at her.

Rachel nodded.

Dylan yanked on the knob—*open*—and he burst inside. Rachel was right beside him. They went in with their weapons up, and they cleared the place, room by room.

Jack wasn't there.

No one was.

Rachel paused beside Dylan's bed. Her feet crunched on broken glass. She frowned. The glass was there, but she didn't know where it had come from. "Dylan…?"

"He's gone." He yanked out his phone and then, barely two seconds later, he said, "Thomas, he's not up here. Start sweeping the perimeter because he couldn't have gone far, not yet."

Rachel backed away from the bed as Dylan kept giving his orders. When he ended the call with Thomas, Dylan contacted the EOD office and asked for a forensics team to meet at his place.

But Rachel doubted the team would find any fingerprints on the scene. Jack was too good to leave any traces behind. She turned away, determined to go and help Thomas with his search.

"No." Dylan's sharp voice stopped her.

She glanced back.

"Not without me," he said. "The guy's close, too close, and he's playing with us."

A break-in at her place. A break-in at his. Rachel wasn't sure that Jack was playing with them, though. "I think he's researching us."

A faint line appeared between Dylan's dark brows.

"It's what he does," Rachel continued. She'd made it her mission to learn as much as she possibly could about Jack and his victims. "He researches his prey. Learns their weaknesses, and then he goes in for the kill."

It wasn't just a game to Jack.

It was life...and death.

Chapter Three

Rachel held her body perfectly still as she sat in the conference room at the EOD. Bruce Mercer had just walked into the room. She figured the EOD boss was pushing sixty, but he was still completely fit and incredibly intimidating.

He'd intimidated Rachel from the first moment she'd met him. According to the whispers she'd heard, Mercer was the man pulling the strings in D.C. He knew all the secrets the politicians wanted to keep hidden, and he could expose those secrets at any time.

But Mercer wasn't the only one to enter that conference room. Noelle Evers followed him inside.

Rachel tried not to let her surprise show. Noelle Evers—*Dr.* Noelle Evers—wasn't EOD. Or at least she hadn't been. A few months ago, Noelle had come in to do some freelance profiling work for Mercer. Noelle normally worked for the FBI. She was supposed to be one of the best when it came to creating criminal profiles.

Mercer had originally used Noelle in an attempt to catch a rogue agent at the EOD. Noelle had created a profile to lead them all to the killer.

But that case is over, so why is Noelle still here?

Rachel was seated between Thomas and Dylan. Mercer

and Noelle settled in the chairs across from them. Rachel noticed that Noelle's hazel gaze darted toward Thomas.

A quick glance showed Rachel that Thomas's stare was locked right on the profiler.

Interesting. Thomas didn't make a habit of showing obvious interest in anyone or anything.

"Our security team finished their sweeps." Mercer's voice filled the room. He had that kind of voice. Strong. A little *too* loud. He was obviously used to barking orders. It was only too easy for Rachel to imagine Mercer as a drill sergeant. She'd bet a hundred bucks he had been at one time.

"The guy knows his B and E," Mercer continued. "No prints, no trace evidence at your place, Rachel."

She'd expected that.

Mercer's focus shifted to Dylan. "But it looks as if things got a little more personal for him at your place."

Wait, what was that supposed to mean?

Then Mercer reached into a small briefcase and pulled out an evidence bag. He pushed a frame across the table at them. "Unless you're the one who smashed this picture, Agent Foxx?"

Rachel leaned forward to get a better view of the framed image. It was a photo of her and Dylan. It had been taken after their mission in Panama last year. They'd been so happy to get the hostages out of that place alive.

"No." Dylan's voice was clipped. "I didn't smash it."

"I figured you hadn't, but I needed to be sure." Mercer left the frame on the table. A few shards of broken glass remained on top of the photo. "We found it inside your nightstand drawer."

"That's where it usually is," Dylan said. Again, his words were clipped.

Rachel's gaze jumped to him. He kept a photo of them in his bedroom?

Dylan didn't look her way, so Rachel glanced toward Mercer and Noelle once more.

Noelle's gaze was studying her. Rachel didn't like that particular look from the profiler. It made her feel a little too much like a bug under a microscope.

"I hoped Jack had cut himself on the glass, but…" Mercer exhaled on a long sigh. "No such luck. No doubt he was wearing gloves. The gloves would explain why there were no prints and no blood."

"We were just minutes behind him," Thomas said. He gave a disgusted shake of his head. "But he still just disappeared."

"He's good at that," Mercer replied. "Too good." Then he glanced over at Noelle. "And that's why we have to *make* him come out into the open."

Rachel had known this would be coming. Mercer's bait plan, no doubt. He'd want to use her—

"Agent Foxx, you're going to draw Jack out for us."

"What?" Rachel's voice rose with her surprise. Dylan wasn't supposed to be bait. He *couldn't* be bait.

But Dylan just nodded and said, "Bring it."

No, no, this was *not* happening.

Her hand slammed down on the table. "You all don't understand—"

"Actually," Mercer said, cutting through her angry words, "I think I do. And Noelle, here, she's very good at predicting what killers will do. She *understands* them particularly well."

Noelle gave a firm nod. The light reflected off the

lenses of her glasses. "He isn't going to kill you, Rachel. You don't have to worry about that."

A laugh escaped her. A broken, twisted laugh. "Really? He's not? Because when he drugged me, tied me up and *shot* me before, I certainly got the impression that Jack wanted me dead."

Noelle held her stare. There was sympathy in the profiler's gaze. "I'm very sorry for what happened to you, but—and this *isn't* to make light of the situation in any way—"

Was the woman serious? Rachel's hands balled into fists in her lap.

"But if Jack had truly wanted to kill you, then why didn't he just slit your throat while he had you tied up?"

Dylan stiffened.

"Or he could have aimed for your heart when he shot you," Noelle continued. "But he didn't. He hit your shoulder. A flesh wound. He's suspected in dozens of kills, so we know he's a professional. I just don't…I don't believe a professional would ever make a mistake like that." A brief pause. "Unless he *wanted* to make that mistake."

A dull ringing filled Rachel's ears. "You're saying he let me live."

"Yes."

"He *kidnapped* me."

Noelle's lips pressed together for a moment, then she softly said, "Perhaps he thought that he *could* go through with the hit on you. But then something changed. Maybe it was seeing you, helpless, realizing that he held the power over you. For men like him, everything is about power."

Rachel's nails bit deeper into her palms.

"He *didn't* kill you when he had the chance." Noelle's shoulders straightened. "And I don't believe that he is back to kill you now."

This was crazy. So much for Noelle being some kind of expert who could peer into a killer's mind. "Jack said he'd come back—"

"But I don't think he meant to kill you. I think...I believe—" now Noelle's voice strengthened as she continued "—he told you that he'd come back...because he wants to be with you."

Rachel could only shake her head.

"But there's a problem," Noelle said. Her gaze swept over to Dylan. "You're the problem, Agent Foxx. You're the man standing between Jack and the woman that he wants." Noelle bent over the table and her finger—tipped with light pink polish—hovered over the frame. "You're the man he sees as his competition for Rachel. And you're the man that he will try and eliminate."

Rachel shot to her feet. "No. *No.*"

All eyes were on her now.

Good. They needed to listen very carefully to her. "I get that you've got a fistful of degrees that tell you how to play mind games, Dr. Evers."

Noelle tensed. "I don't consider them games at all."

Rachel wasn't so sure. "But you don't know Jack. *I* don't even know him, and I dated the man for three months." Months that seemed like a dream to her now. No, not a dream, a nightmare. "He isn't in town to make some kind of love connection with me. He *killed* Hank Patterson. Jack is in town to take care of his usual business—death." That had to be obvious to everyone.

"He might have come to D.C. because he had a hit," Mercer agreed, "but that doesn't explain why he went

to your place or to Dylan's." His fingers tapped on the
table's edge. "I'm actually surprised that Dylan came
up on his radar, but then, if Jack has been keeping track
of you—"

"And I think he has," Noelle said.

"Then he'd know that you and Dylan are…close."

"We aren't dating!" Okay, yes, she was definitely
flushing as she said that line.

"But Jack believes you are." Now Noelle cocked her
head as her gaze slid between them. "The picture he
discovered of you two will be the evidence he needs to
cement that belief in his head."

And, if Jack had been watching her last night, then
he would've seen Dylan kiss her, too. They'd been right
there in the street. Her nervous gaze flew over to Dylan.
He wasn't looking at her. Just staring straight at Mercer.

A soldier, awaiting his orders.

But the orders could get him *killed.*

"The fact that he broke into Dylan's home works for
us," Mercer said. "It shows that he still has a connection
to you, Rachel, and that he doesn't like it that another
man is close to you."

Her breath was coming too fast. Rachel tried to ease
the panting as she held tightly to her control. "He could
be planning other hits," Rachel said. "We need to work
on that angle for tracking him down. We need to find
out why he went after Patterson—"

"And we will," Mercer said. "You, Foxx and Thomas
Anthony will run down those leads."

Now that was something that she could work with.
She could—

"You and Foxx are to stay close to one another at all
times," Mercer added with a stern stare. "The closer

that you two are, then the more likely Jack will make an attack on Foxx."

She was still on her feet, and Mercer, apparently, was still insane. "You're wrong about Jack." Mercer was wrong. The profiler was wrong. Jack wasn't keeping her alive because of some emotional connection he felt to her.

He could kill her at any time. *But I'm harder to kill now. Dylan taught me how to be even stronger.*

Mercer just shrugged. "If I'm wrong, then he'll come to kill you. And in that case—well, Dylan will be there. I'm covering my bases, Agent Mancini. I'm doing my best to keep all of my agents alive, and I *will* bring down this SOB before he has the chance to escape the country again."

Tension had Rachel's muscles trembling.

"That's it for now," Mercer said, his voice lowering. "Now let's get to work and *find Jack.*"

Rachel headed for the door. Thomas was at her side.

"Ah, Agent Foxx?" Mercer said. "A moment, please."

Rachel looked back. She did *not* like the expression in Mercer's eyes.

And the determination on Dylan's face chilled her.

THE DOOR CLOSED behind Rachel and Thomas. Dylan remained in his seat, with his gaze on Mercer. Noelle was still with the director, and the glance she threw his way held more than a hint of nervousness.

Ah, so Noelle wasn't exactly game-on for whatever plan Mercer was about to spill.

"I expected Rachel to be...hesitant," Mercer began.

Dylan let his brows lift.

"But we can use your relationship with Mancini."

Mercer gave a firm nod. "It's the most obvious tool that we have."

Keeping the emotion out of his voice, Dylan asked, "Just what sort of relationship do you think I have with Rachel? Team members working in the field aren't allowed to have…physical relationships." That was the spiel they'd all been given when they joined the EOD.

"It's not what I think that matters." Mercer's lips curled in the faintest of smiles. "It's what Jack thinks. Rachel is the only emotional connection we know that the man has—"

"He may not have even realized that he *could* connect with someone." Noelle spoke up as she slid off her glasses. "Not until he found her. And his connection to Rachel isn't exactly the way a normal man would feel. It's not, of course, the way that you feel—"

Dylan held up his hand. "Neither of you know anything about my feelings for Rachel."

Noelle bit her lip.

Mercer just kept that faint smile on his face, then after a moment he inclined his head. "I know enough to realize that you'll get the job done, won't you? I believe your words were, 'Bring it', yes?"

Hell, yes. He wanted Jack to come his way. Because Dylan didn't want Rachel afraid any longer. He knew she still looked over her shoulder, wondering when Jack might strike. She wasn't going to be safe again, not until Jack was contained.

Or killed.

"It's the appearance that matters," Mercer told him. "Give Jack the appearance necessary to push him over the edge. Let him think that you and Rachel are lovers."

His back teeth were grinding together. "What if this

BS plan of yours backfires? What if he doesn't come after me? What if he goes after Rachel?"

"Like I said before, that's why the two of you are working so closely. You'll guard her back. She'll watch yours. That is the way things worked for you and Agent Mancini on your other missions."

Yes, it was.

Noelle shifted slightly in her chair. "And Agent Anthony will be there, covering you both."

Dylan glanced down at his hands. Rachel's fingers had been clenched into tight fists. Her knuckles had been white as tension coursed through her body. He'd wanted to stroke her shoulder, to soothe her, but he hadn't reached out to Rachel. Not with Mercer and Noelle watching them so closely.

"The EOD has taken a very personal interest in Jack."

Dylan looked up at those low words. Mercer's smile was gone.

"That interest isn't just because of Agent Mancini, though I hope you know how much I value her." Mercer stood. His chair rolled back behind him. "Jack has been killing for ten years. The very first man that he killed— the first we linked him to, anyway—worked in my military unit. Carson George survived wars, enemy camps and flat-out hell, only to be taken down in his own apartment just outside D.C."

Dylan had read all of the files on Jack. "He always goes after military, either currently enlisted personnel or retired members." No civilians, ever.

Why?

Noelle cleared her throat. "I think he's ex-military, too. And he sees his victims...he sees them as more of a challenge. Going after civilians would be too easy, and Jack isn't for easy."

No, he was for blood. For death.

"I've known several of his victims. They were good men and women. Jack has to be stopped." Mercer nodded toward Noelle. "The FBI is after him, too, so watch your step."

"I have…associates who are eager to close in on him," Noelle explained carefully.

"One way or another, we *will* take Jack down." Mercer was adamant. "But I don't want to lose any of my team members in this hunt."

Rachel would not be lost. "Understood, sir."

"Good." Flat. "I knew I could count on you."

Mercer and Noelle filed out of the room.

Dylan remained seated. Count on him? To take out Jack?

With pleasure.

BEFORE HIS DEATH, Hank Patterson had been planning to rule on a court-martial for Lance Corporal Chris Harris, a man who'd been accused of attacking a fellow marine—that marine had wound up in the hospital with three broken ribs and a broken arm.

Mercer had pulled strings and gotten Rachel and Dylan access to Chris Harris. A military guard was stationed a few feet away from the prisoner, and they were in a small, narrow room at the military holding facility.

Chris Harris, barely twenty-two, wore a smirk on his face as he glanced at Rachel and Dylan. "What do you two want?" His gaze drifted over them. "You're not officers…"

"Not anymore," Dylan agreed. He didn't sit. Neither

did Rachel. She was too tense to stay still, so she paced toward the left wall and prepared to watch the show.

When it came to interrogations, Dylan had a gift.

"If you're not officers, then who are you?" Chris glanced at her. His eyes were a dull blue, his cheeks ruddy. And his hands were moving nervously against the table.

"We're friends...of Hank Patterson's," Dylan answered.

Chris's lips trembled. Rachel was staring right at him when he made that telling movement. *The guy almost smiled.* She was sure of it.

Dylan's hands slapped down on the table in front of Chris. *Dylan saw that movement, too.* "You know he's dead."

Chris nodded. "Real shame." His voice said it was anything *but* a shame. "My lawyer...he's checking things for me now."

"Yeah, I'm sure he is. I heard the trial wasn't going so well for you."

Chris shrugged. "Don't think that matters now, does it? New trial, new judge."

Dylan stared at him. "You're sweating, Chris."

"It's hot in here."

"No, it's not..." Dylan glanced toward the guard, gave a nod.

The guard turned his back.

"Why's he doing that?"

The guard walked away.

"Hey! Wait!" Chris yelled.

"He's not going to wait. And you know what else, Chris? There's not going to be any record of this little visit today..."

Chris gulped.

"Hank Patterson had a lot of powerful friends."

"He was railroading me! He kept me locked up in here the whole time when I should've been out! My lawyer's gonna get me out now—"

Dylan just kept his dark gaze focused on the prisoner.

"The guy thought I was guilty from the first minute I stepped into that courtroom! He didn't give me a chance—"

"So you made sure that he wouldn't be around long, didn't you? You made your own *chance*."

"I didn't do anything!" Chris rocked back in his chair. "The guy got attacked. He died. Sucks, but that's life."

No, it wasn't. "He had a family," Rachel said. An image of Patterson's body flashed through her mind. "A daughter. A son." His wife had died years before.

"I got a family, too," Chris snapped. "You think my old man likes that I wound up like this? He was military, too. Thirty years. Hell, *no,* this shouldn't have happened, but that lying jerk McAlister said I got drunk and roughed up some girls. I didn't. *He* did. McAlister's ribs got broken because I was making him back off. That's what happened." His chin jerked into the air. "I should get a medal. Instead, they threw me into the brig."

"I don't care about your sob story," Dylan fired out.

Chris blinked.

"I want to know how you found him." Dylan pointed at Chris. "And you're going to tell me."

Chris laughed. "You're crazy."

"The FBI is checking your father's bank account right now," Dylan revealed. Rachel knew that the EOD was actually the one doing the check. "Are they going to see that it's short by…oh, maybe twenty thousand? Thirty? That used to be Jack's going rate."

Chris's smile dimmed. "I don't know any Jack."

"Sure you do. You had him kill Hank Patterson."

Chris's gaze cut over to Rachel. "Pretty lady, are you just gonna stand there and let your—"

"Eyes here," Dylan snarled.

Chris jerked upright. His eyes flew back to Dylan.

"I'm not your lawyer." Dylan's words hit with a thundering intensity. "I'm not one of your guards. I don't care about how much money your father has or who the hell he served with. I'm an ex-SEAL, and I am your worst nightmare." He leaned toward Chris. "You think you're safe in here? I've got you now. No guards will hear you if you cry out. No one will hear you but me."

"I didn't hire Jack!"

"You're weak." Disgust was heavy in Dylan's voice. "The bully who picks on others, but never on anyone that he thinks can actually fight back against him."

Chris's lips clamped together.

"You knew Patterson was going to rule against you, so you had him killed. Probably you and your old man."

Goose bumps rose on Rachel's arms. This was just like before. Her last case as a Marine Corps Judge Advocate. Jack had been brought in on that case, too…

"Money can't buy everything," Dylan said. His eyes were like black ice. "And it's sure not going to buy you freedom. You're going to stay locked up, and everyone will know just what a weakling you are—"

Chris erupted from his chair. "I'm not weak!" He flew right over the table, tackling Dylan. The two men slammed to the floor.

Rachel lunged forward.

But she didn't need to help Dylan. He'd already tossed Chris off him and Dylan was back on his feet. "Wrong move, kid," Dylan snarled.

Breath heaving, Chris glared at him. "No, *you* made the wrong move. I can make you vanish. Make you disappear, just like I did Patterson—"

And there it was. The confession that they'd wanted. Dylan had just needed to push the guy past his control in order to get the words that they wanted to hear.

"One call is all I need to make to my old man act. Just *one.*" Even as he spit out the last word, Chris's eyes widened, but it was too late. His fury had driven him to reveal too much.

"Thanks, genius," Dylan drawled mockingly. "That was all I wanted to know." He turned away and glanced at Rachel. "Ready?"

Because now the trail would take them to Chris's father. "Definitely."

"No!" Chris yelled. "Hell, *no!* You aren't going to keep me in here!" His eyes were wild. "I've got plans. *One way or another, I'm getting out of here! I won't stand trial again—I'm getting out.*"

"No," Dylan flatly told him, "you're not. You won't be free anytime soon."

Chris screamed and ran forward again. Never taking his eyes off Rachel, Dylan struck out with his right hand. When Chris hit the floor, he was out cold. "Now let's get out of here," Dylan said. He headed for the door. The guard appeared because he'd never gone far, not really.

"It was all recorded?" Rachel asked because she had to be sure. After what Chris had done, she wanted him to pay for Patterson's death. Just as Jack would pay.

The guard nodded.

Rachel glanced back at Chris. The guy wasn't moving. She hoped Chris got used to being locked up because he wouldn't be a free man again.

THE SUNLIGHT BEAT DOWN on Dylan as they left the military holding facility. They'd cleared all the guard checkpoints and already phoned in their intel to the EOD.

He opened the door for Rachel, and she slid inside the car. His ride this time, not Thomas's. A vehicle that came courtesy of the EOD. A tracking device was included with the car so that the other EOD agents could always locate the vehicle.

In an organization like the EOD, you could never be too careful.

His hand went to the ignition, but then Dylan paused. He shot a fast glance at Rachel. "Are you going to say anything?"

She blinked at him. The sunlight streamed through the window, making her skin appear so golden. Rachel was Italian, part of a big, brimming family. A family that thought she worked as a pencil pusher for Uncle Sam. They had no idea what Rachel really did for a living. If they knew, he was sure they'd be terrified.

Dylan didn't have to worry about his own family being terrified. He had no family. His folks had passed when he was nineteen and, unlike Rachel, he didn't have any brothers or sisters.

Actually…Rachel was the only family he had. The thought slipped through his mind. *I'm not alone because I have Rachel.*

"I was certain you'd get the intel from him," she said with a shrug. "You're good at your job."

Dylan grunted and still didn't start the vehicle. "I'm

not talking about the interrogation. I'm talking about what went down with Mercer earlier." They'd left the EOD without discussing that little meeting, and he wasn't going to hold off any longer. They needed to clear the air.

She held his gaze. "I don't…" Her words trailed away and she hesitated before saying, "You know I don't like the plan. And I think Mercer and Noelle are wrong. Jack doesn't have an attachment to me. He just wants me dead."

"If that were the case…" The words were brutal, but they had to be said. "Then why aren't you in the ground?" *Don't think of her that way. Don't.*

She flinched. "Start the car, Dylan."

He didn't. "Noelle knows her killers. That's the point of her being a profiler, right?" Dylan pressed. "She says that he has a connection to you. I believe her. We need to use that connection."

"What they want to use is *you,* not me. They want to dangle you in front of Jack like—like you're a red flag hanging in front of a bull."

"So what? I've been used on missions before. I'm an agent. That's just part of my job." Risk. Danger. The adrenaline rush. It was his nine-to-five routine. *More like my 24/7 routine.*

"They want him to think that we're lovers." Now her voice was hushed and her eyes were troubled. "They want you to pretend to be involved with me."

He had to handle this carefully. "It's not exactly a hardship to do that."

Her lips parted.

"I've done jobs much worse."

And he'd just said the wrong thing. So much for being

careful. Dylan knew he'd bungled when her eyes narrowed to chips of blue fire.

"Oh, so glad that I don't fall into the category of *worse* for you," Rachel snapped. "I mean, I'd hate for the idea of being my lover to be so terrible for you to consider. I don't want to give you nightmares or anything."

"It's not terrible." His voice was low. "It's tempting."

She tensed.

Time for them both to cut through the lies. "You have to know," Dylan told her, aware that a new intensity had entered his voice. "You have to know how I feel."

She glanced away.

No, he wasn't having that. He caught her chin and made her look at him. "Come on, Rachel, it's me. *Three years.* I've been with you, at your side for three long years."

She didn't speak.

"I want you." The words were a growling rumble. He'd meant them to come out easier, without that hard edge, but when it came to Rachel and his need for her, there was very little control there for him. "I've held back because I didn't know what *you* wanted."

She still wasn't speaking.

Hell, he should have just kept his mouth shut. He'd thought Rachel might want him, too. Especially after the way she'd kissed him the other night.

I thought wrong.

He freed her chin and turned away from her. His fingers curled around the key and he twisted it in the ignition. The car immediately snarled to life.

Rachel's hand flew out. Her fingers clamped around his. "I want you to be safe. I don't…I don't ever want extra danger to come your way because of me."

Her touch electrified him. If he ever actually got her naked and beneath him the way that Dylan wanted…

I won't let her go.

He swallowed and tried to keep some of the need from his voice as he told her, "Baby, I'm EOD. Danger is just a way of life for me." His gaze cut to her.

Her eyes were on him.

"What do you *want?*" Dylan pushed. He waited, needing her to say…

"I want you." Her words were so quiet that he had to strain in order to hear them.

And as soon as he did hear them, everything changed for Dylan.

He turned fully toward her. Arousal had flooded through him at her soft words. He didn't want to be in that car then. He wanted to take Rachel away from that place. He wanted to get lost *in* her.

Rachel's thick lashes lowered. "But you're my closest friend, Dylan. The only man that I truly trust. I don't want to lose you."

"You won't." His promise.

She licked her lips.

And Dylan couldn't take any more. He pulled her as close as he could get her and his mouth took hers.

The kiss was hard, deep and he knew that the lust he felt for Rachel wasn't going to be contained, not any longer.

For three years, he'd played by the rules. Been the good guy.

He was tired of being good. Rachel was about to learn just how far he would be willing to go in order to have her.

I will do anything.

Her mouth opened beneath his. Her nails sank into his shoulders as she held him just as tightly as he held her. Her taste was as addictive as before, driving him wild. His tongue thrust into her mouth, and arousal flooded through him as he tasted her. Her taste was both rich and sweet, and he wanted *more.*

But not here. Not now.

Dylan let the kiss linger just a few moments more. Because he had to *take* more.

But then he pulled back. Damn reluctantly. Her cheeks were flushed. Her eyes gleamed.

"There's no going back now," he warned her.

Rachel's breath rushed out. "I should be saying that to you. You're the one walking into danger."

He was ready for it. She needed to be ready for what was coming, too.

"It's not…not just part of a cover, is it?" Rachel asked him.

That question had anger piercing through him. *"No."*

"Because I need honesty between us. No matter what."

He nodded. "And you know what I need?" The gloves were off.

"What?" A whisper from her.

"You. Naked. Beneath me."

He saw her pupils spread. Her breathing kicked up a little more.

"And I'll have that," Dylan promised her.

JACK WHISTLED AS he headed up the stone steps that would take him to his prey.

An old acquaintance, one who'd called him back to town.

Jack knocked on the door. He waved to the nosy neighbor across the street. She waved back.

He didn't worry about the woman being able to identify him. He had on a baseball cap. A loose sweatshirt. Jogging shorts. He looked like any of the other dozen joggers currently running down the street.

Only there was one major difference between them.

He was there to kill. Not to jog.

The door opened. William "Billy" Harris stood there, his eyes wide. "Who the hell are you?" Billy demanded. "What do you want?"

Ah, even his old mentor didn't recognize him. It was amazing how time—and a little surgery—could change a man. Jack reached into his pocket and pulled out a playing card. "I'm here to finish our business."

Billy's eyes widened. *"Jack?"*

Billy had been the one to first give him that moniker. They'd been playing cards. The pot had been up to three hundred dollars. Billy had been holding three tens.

But I held all the Jacks.

He smiled and stepped forward. Billy immediately fell back. Jack closed the door. There was only so much that he wanted the nosy neighbor to see.

"I...I can't believe you answered my email," Billy said as he ran a shaking hand over his head. Billy hadn't aged so well. He'd once been a fierce soldier, a leader.

Now his hands shook and his shoulders slumped. The paunch near his middle said the guy didn't exactly keep up his old exercise routine.

Ah, Billy, I expected more from you.

"It was a shot in the dark," Billy muttered. "But I was desperate."

Desperate men would do anything.

Jack shrugged. "I was due a visit back here." *Rachel waited here.* As did other, new business. Lately, it seemed that Jack's services were in particularly high demand.

Soon I'll move on to my next target. A very big kill. Perhaps the most challenging one of his career.

Yet for now, he had to take care of his current payday and his prey. "You know why I'm here, Billy. I did my part, and you owe me."

Billy nodded quickly. "I'll just go get the rest of your cash."

Normally, Jack didn't conduct his transactions in person. For Billy, he'd made a special exception. He'd let the guy wire half of the payment to him, the upfront money. And Jack had agreed to collect the remainder due in D.C. *after* the kill had been completed.

Silently, he followed Billy down the narrow hallway.

He knew Billy very well. After all, Billy had been the one to turn him on to this line of work.

The government trained us to kill. Why not use our skills? They're just going to dump us, to forget us. I say we make sure no one can ever forget just who we are!

Billy had been drunk at the time and furious over a demotion.

Jack hadn't been drunk. He'd been fully aware. He'd seen an opportunity. He'd taken it.

I get to pick my kills now. And I get paid for it.

The money had never been sweeter.

Billy stood in front of his wall safe. He spun the dial, and it snicked open. The cash was in there.

So was a gun.

Jack could see the edge of the weapon. And Billy, well, the fool was reaching for it.

And that's one of the reasons why you are my prey today.

Before Billy could swing around with that gun, Jack grabbed the man, and he slammed Billy's head into the side of the safe. "Wrong move," Jack whispered. Then he snatched up the gun.

So convenient…it even had a silencer attached.

Billy slumped to the floor. Jack put the gun to his head. "Did you truly think you were going to be able to double-cross me?"

Billy had busted his lip when he'd careened into the safe. Blood dripped from the wound.

"I've been at this game a long time now. You aren't the first to have this idiotic idea." Jack shrugged. "But guess what happens to people who try to play me." His fingers tightened around the trigger.

Billy shook his head, frantic. "I wasn't going to shoot you! It was just for protection, just in case—"

"In case a killer came calling?" He wasn't in the mood to waste any more time. "Goodbye, Billy."

"No!"

Just as Billy screamed, a loud pounding echoed through the house—a pounding against the front door of Billy's home.

Billy's eyes bulged. *"Help me!"* he screamed as he lunged to the side. *"Help—"*

Jack fired.

Chapter Four

"Help me!"

Dylan's gaze jerked to meet Rachel's when he heard the scream, then they moved as one, and they kicked in the door to William Harris's home.

Dylan heard the thud of footsteps, running fast and to the left, going toward the back of the house. He raced ahead, following that sound, and he nearly tripped over the body on the floor.

One glance and he knew it was William Harris. The guy looked just like the photo that had been sent from the EOD. Only in that photo, William hadn't been bleeding from a gushing wound in his chest.

Rachel knelt on the floor, moving in close beside the injured man. Dylan heard her calling for backup and ordering an ambulance to the address.

Dylan didn't think an ambulance would be able to do much good. William's shirt was soaking with blood before his eyes.

"Tried to...get away..." William's voice rasped out. "Still shot me...chest...not...head..."

Dylan pinned Rachel with his stare. "You stay with him."

Her eyes widened. "Dylan, you can't—"

He couldn't let Jack get away. Dylan lunged toward the back of the house. Jack only had a lead of a few minutes.

Dylan's hand slapped against the back door, and the old wood swung open. Dylan jumped onto the narrow patio. His gaze swept to the left.

He saw a man scaling a fence. Tall, broad shoulders, wearing a baseball cap, jogging shorts and a sweatshirt.

And gloves.

Dylan knew he was looking at Jack. "Stop!" Dylan yelled.

Of course, the guy didn't slow down for a second. He heaved over the edge of the fence and ran.

Swearing, Dylan pumped his legs and headed for the tall chain-link fence.

"Look at me," Rachel said as William Harris's blood coated her fingers. The wound was bad. So very bad. The ambulance was en route, but Rachel didn't think it was going to arrive in time.

William blinked. His face was already ashen.

"Tell me who did this to you." Because he didn't have much time left to talk. He was their main lead right then. They needed William to hang on.

His throat worked, but no words came from his mouth.

"We know you hired him to kill Patterson. But he turned on you, didn't he?" She'd seen the safe. Its door still hung open. "What if he decides to turn on your son, too? Do you want Chris to die?" It was the only card she had to play.

William's lips moved.

She put her ear next to his mouth, struggling to hear what he said.

"J...Jack..."

Her stomach tightened. "I want his real name. Do you know it? Can you tell me?"

"P-played me..." The words broke on a gasp.

I'm losing him.

"Please!" Her head lifted just a few inches. She wanted to stare into his eyes, but his eyes were shut. "Help me to find him! He shot you..."

"My...own...g-gun... Almost...g-got h-him..."

So he'd been planning to kill Jack?

One double cross for another.

In the distance, she heard the scream of a siren. "The ambulance is so close," she told him. "Just fight. Hang on."

His breath slid out. "Not...en-enough..."

No, the ambulance wasn't close enough.

"Taught him...t-taught Jack...all..."

He didn't say more. His chest wasn't rising any longer.

"William? *William?*" Her knees shifted as she edged closer to him, and that was when she saw the playing card that had been under his right arm.

A bloody Jack of Hearts.

DYLAN FOLLOWED JACK, keeping his eyes on the baseball cap as the man weaved and dodged through the city.

The killer had dropped some cash in his frantic run. Dylan hadn't stopped to pick it up. He didn't care about the money. Only Jack.

The baseball cap vanished as the guy rounded a corner.

With a burst of speed, Dylan rounded that same corner and found himself in an alley.

There was no sign of Jack. *He has to be here, though.* Dylan's gaze scanned the perimeter. There was no way that Jack had just vanished.

He advanced slowly. The alley stank of rotten food. There was a big garbage container to the right. And the back entrance to a restaurant was just a few steps away from that bin.

Did you think you could escape in there?

Dylan hurried forward. He yanked open that back door. Saw no one. Dylan advanced. When he burst into the kitchen with his gun drawn, a chorus of shouts and screams met his arrival.

All of the kitchen staff members were wearing white uniforms. They stared at him with fear and horror on their faces.

"Where the hell is he?" Dylan demanded.

His question was answered with more frantic shouts. He pulled out his ID, the nice, fake FBI ID that usually gave him a free pass in situations like this one. "I'm following a suspect. White male, six foot two, two hundred pounds. He was wearing a blue sweatshirt, jogging shorts and a baseball cap." His gaze lasered around the room. "Where the hell did he go?"

But no one knew. They all said they'd seen nothing. No one...but Dylan.

Vanished.

Rage twisted inside him.

DYLAN BRAKED HIS CAR in front of Rachel's apartment building. Fury still rode him.

Fury and fear.

"I don't think you should stay here tonight," he said as he glanced over at her. Actually, Dylan figured that staying at her place was one damn bad idea. "He's already broken into your place once."

"And yours," Rachel pointed out as she tilted her head to study him. "Besides, Thomas is watching the street in front of my apartment. He's got guard duty. And Mercer told me that the EOD upgraded my security system."

Yeah, they had. He killed the engine. "If you're staying here, then so am I." He had a duffel bag in his trunk, one that he kept ready because he never knew when the EOD would ship him out on a mission.

"You don't…you don't have to do that. I told you, Thomas has guard duty. I don't need—"

"Maybe it's about what I need." And he *needed* to be close to her. "Besides, isn't the master plan for the guy to think that we're lovers? I doubt that he'll buy the charade if we're sleeping across the city from each other."

Her lashes lowered. Night had fallen on the city, and the only light in the car came from the streetlamp a few feet away. That wasn't nearly enough illumination to let him read her expression, and he sure wanted to know what she was thinking.

"A charade?" Rachel whispered. "Is that all it will be?"

The memory of their kiss—the kiss they'd had in that car—was suddenly right between them, he knew it was. He didn't need to see her expression any longer.

But he did have to tread very carefully. "We can be whatever you want us to be." It had to be her choice, he knew that. But once she did make the choice…

You choose me, then, baby, you will be mine.

"Let's talk upstairs, then." She fumbled with the door handle and hurriedly exited the vehicle.

He followed her. And he grabbed the duffel bag from

the back of the car. His gaze trekked down the street. The pub was already busy. That place *usually* was, from what he'd seen. But he wouldn't be going in that pub searching for Rachel that night.

I've got her. And I'm not letting her go. Because he knew the truth now. Rachel wanted him as badly as he wanted her.

He put his hand at her back, then headed into the building with her. For anyone watching, it would look like they were just two lovers, heading in for the night.

They didn't speak as they climbed the stairs. Rachel unlocked her door then reset the new alarm system. She turned toward him, and he caught the flash of worry on her face. "I have to check and make sure that he hasn't been here…"

But Dylan was already moving. He dropped the duffel bag on the floor and went straight to her bedroom.

The covers weren't disturbed this time. No playing card waited for her.

He heard her soft exhale behind him, and he turned back to look at her. Some of the tension had eased from Rachel's shoulders.

If he could, he'd take away all her fear and worry.

I will. When I take out Jack.

"I need to shower," Rachel murmured. She stared down at her hands now. "I just…I washed the blood away, but I can still feel it on me."

He nodded. Dylan understood exactly what Rachel meant. He'd been there before on plenty of other missions. He also knew that while it was easy to wash the blood away, the memory wouldn't fade anytime soon.

"William Harris hired Jack to kill Patterson. I know

he wasn't an innocent but…" She swallowed. "I wish things could've ended differently for him."

So did Dylan. He could have made William Harris talk. They would have been closer to unmasking Jack. Instead—

He slipped away from me again.

Dylan cleared his throat. "Go shower. I'll wait for you in the den." Because if he stood there in her bedroom, with her scent around him any longer, he was going to crack.

He'd take her in his arms.

He'd kiss her.

He'd make her *his.*

Dylan slipped past her. The image of Rachel wet, naked, in that shower was already making the tension flood through his body. He was so close to the one thing he wanted most. So close.

"Dylan…"

He stopped at her door. His hand curled around the door frame, his knuckles whitening. "Shower first," he said, and was surprised by the gravel-roughness of his voice. "Then…"

Then I'm taking you.

He didn't say that. But maybe, maybe he didn't have to.

Dylan stalked out of the room before his control shredded. He wanted to be *in* that shower with her, but after what had happened, he knew she'd need a few minutes to herself. A man had died right in front of her. Hell, yes, that would shake anyone up—even a woman as tough as Rachel.

He found himself in her den. Pacing. A fast glance at the clock showed him that it was nearing 10:00 p.m.

And Rachel hasn't eaten. The sudden thought shot through his head.

He stilled. He hadn't eaten. She hadn't. They'd been too busy at the crime scene. Too busy chasing leads that hadn't taken them to Jack.

He could hear the roar of the shower. Rachel was in there. Naked. *Wet.*

He swallowed. She had to be starving. And, for what he wanted to happen between them that night, the woman would need her strength.

The kitchen wasn't exactly his area of expertise, so Dylan entered the room cautiously. When it came to cooking, he was woefully behind Rachel. The woman usually took pity on him. She'd bring over dinner to his place at least three times a week. Lasagna or her killer spaghetti. Garlic bread that melted in his mouth.

He opened her refrigerator. It wasn't going to be pretty and it sure wouldn't be up to Rachel's usual standards, but he'd have a meal ready for her by the time she exited the shower.

DYLAN FOXX WOULD DIE.

Jack stared at the lights in Rachel's apartment. That guy was up there with her.

Jack should have been the one with Rachel. He was the one she loved. Not the EOD agent.

The EOD. They'd been a thorn in his side for too long. They actually thought they could stop him? *Him?* He was unstoppable. A force of nature.

The government had made him, honed him. Now he was the perfect killing machine.

And I'm ready to kill.

He knew there was a guard outside Rachel's apartment building. Tagging the guy had been easy, even though the agent did a decent job of sticking to the shadows.

I'm a step ahead.

Always.

He didn't need to get inside Rachel's apartment in order to take out Dylan Foxx. He could take steps for the man's execution from outside.

He just had to plan carefully, had to move all the players right in this little game.

Jack reached into his pocket and pulled out a playing card. The Jack. That card was just for Dylan.

Because you're next.

Jack rarely killed unless money was involved. After all, he wasn't a monster. He was a businessman. Patterson had just been business.

Dylan Foxx…his death would be both for business and for pleasure.

You should've been faster in that alley. If you'd rounded the corner seconds sooner, you would've seen me scaling that restaurant wall.

Dylan Foxx kept underestimating him. That was a fatal mistake.

RACHEL BELTED HER bathrobe around her body. She stared in the mirror. The woman who gazed back at her looked nervous, maybe even afraid. Her eyes were too big. Her lips trembled.

Rachel's hands tightened around the belt. *Get a grip.* Women took lovers every day. Rachel faced down terrorists and madmen on a routine basis. Surely, she had this.

Her breath eased out. She opened the door. Paused. *Dylan matters. I don't want to mess this up.*

Her steps were swallowed by the thick carpeting. She crept toward the den. She'd worked up a semi-speech in the shower. Something that would sound fairly sophisticated. They were friends. Of course they could be lovers, too. They could enjoy one another.

No emotions. Just pleasure. That was the spiel in her mind. It was also a—

Lie, lie, lie. Because when it came to Dylan, her emotions always seemed to be involved.

Mercer had given them the go-ahead for this charade. Only she and Dylan would know that they'd actually carried things to the next level.

When Jack and the threat he posed were gone, would she and Dylan return to a friends-only basis? Or would it be too late for that?

Her gaze darted around the den. Dylan wasn't there. He was—

The smell of scrambled eggs teased her nose. Her head immediately turned toward the kitchen.

Dylan stood behind the counter. He motioned toward the table. "It's not much, but I didn't want you starving on me."

He'd *cooked?* Dylan was the king of takeout. He never cooked.

"Eggs, bread and wine." He gave a little shrug. Was it her imagination or were his cheeks a little ruddy? "I know, it's no Rachel Mancini Italian feast, but it will keep you going through the night."

She found herself smiling. Even after everything that had happened that day, a bubble of happiness pushed through her. Dylan could do that. He could always make her happy, even when she knew she should be afraid.

"It smells wonderful," she replied as she headed toward him.

Dylan's gaze slid down her body, lingering on her legs. The robe was short, falling to only midthigh, and she was pretty sure that his eyes heated as he stared at her.

Her skin sure seemed to burn beneath his gaze.

Very slowly, Dylan's eyes rose to her face once more. "Do you…feel better?"

Rachel nodded.

Dylan walked toward the table. It was a big table, able to hold eight. Whenever her family was in town—usually once a month—they'd get together at her place for a dinner night. The table should have looked too big for an intimate gathering of two.

It didn't. Dylan had two plates set close together on the table. And now, two glasses of wine joined those plates.

He'd even taken out and lit one of her candles. The soft glow chased some of the chill from her. Dylan pulled back her chair. Rachel slid onto the seat, her gaze not able to leave his for long. "I didn't…expect this."

His hand brushed over her shoulder, and Rachel tensed. Just that little touch had her body driving into a hyperawareness of him.

He took his own seat. Dylan drank a sip of wine then, his fingers loose around the stem of the glass, he asked, voice curious, "What did you expect? That I'd tumble you into bed as soon as you stepped out of the bathroom?"

She grabbed for her wine. Took a big, fortifying gulp and replied, honestly, "Yes."

The candlelight seemed to be reflected in his eyes.

His lips—sensual, but with a slightly hard edge—curved faintly. "I'd be lying if I said that thought didn't cross my mind."

She had to take another gulp of her wine. So much for elegant sipping.

"But what I have in mind for us…it's not going to be fast. It's not going to be easy."

Oh…wow.

"The pleasure will last all night. One time with you isn't going to be enough for me."

It sounded as if he was warning her.

He was.

"I've wanted you too long. When I get you beneath me, I won't be letting you go anytime soon."

She'd drained her wine.

That faint grin of his stretched a bit more. "You should eat, Rachel, before the wine goes to your head."

She started eating, but her mind was on what he'd said to her. *On him.* "If you wanted me, why didn't you say something?"

"Because at first, you weren't ready for me." A darker note entered his voice. "Jack made you afraid. You didn't trust any man that you met, not in those early days."

She still didn't trust easily. Rachel put down her fork. "I trust you."

He poured her more wine. "I know." His head cocked as he watched her. "But you haven't told me all of your secrets, have you?"

No. She didn't drink more. Not yet. "And you haven't told me yours." There was a lot she didn't know about him. A lot she hadn't explored before.

"What do you want to know?" He'd finished his food and went back to sipping more wine.

The wine was making it easier for her to ask him. "Your lovers." The words tumbled from her. "I'm going to assume that you've had your share."

A man like him—with that aura of bad-boy danger he carried—had no hard time hooking up with the ladies. She'd witnessed him in action herself. When they'd gone on missions, the women always seemed to flock to Dylan.

"My share," he repeated, nodding faintly. "Don't worry, baby. If you're trying to find out if I know my way around the bedroom, rest assured, I do."

She needed more wine. "I know that." She'd never doubted it for a second. The sensual promise was right there in his eyes. "I, um…" *Tell him.* If they were taking this step, he needed to know her secrets. "I already told you that I didn't sleep with Jack." Her hands slid down and curled in her lap. The silk of her robe brushed lightly against her skin.

"And I'm damn glad to know that."

"But the thing is…I haven't exactly had a lot of lovers in my life." She held his gaze, waiting for his response. If he was expecting some kind of casual sophistication from her about this aspect of their relationship, well…

It won't happen.

He'd better get used to some disappointment on that end. And, despite the little speech she'd planned in the shower, now that the moment was actually at hand, Rachel just couldn't force herself to say those words. That wasn't who she was.

He leaned toward her. "I don't want to know about the lovers from your past. They don't matter anymore."

Oh. "There were only two," she muttered.

His eyes narrowed. "Forget them."

She already had.

"I only want you to think about me tonight. Not about your past. Not about that loser Jack. No one else is here. Just you and just me."

Right. She could do this. She *wanted* to do this. "I've fantasized about you before," Rachel confessed. Her voice had gone husky. "Wondered what it would be like if you—"

Dylan surged to his feet. The back of his chair slammed to the floor and, in the next instant, he'd yanked her out of her chair. His fingers were tight around her arms. "In my dreams, you were in my bed more times than I can count."

Her lips parted in surprise and he kissed her. Not an easy, teasing kiss. Not any kind of getting-to-know-you peck.

This was a full-on, I-want-you-naked-and-I'll-have-you-that-way kiss. His tongue thrust into her mouth. He tasted her. He dominated. He made her toes curl and made her want so much more from him.

Her hands rose and sank into the darkness of his hair. It was so soft against her fingers. A direct contrast to his rock-hard body. There was incredible power in his body. She knew it. She'd sure seen him in action enough times.

He twisted them around, pushing her back against the edge of the table. He tasted of the wine, and his taste was making her feel a rush of euphoria.

Dylan was right. This moment is just about us.

First times with a new lover were supposed to be awkward. Hers sure had been. Fumbling. Hesitations. A woman was supposed to need time in order to get to know her lover.

But…Dylan already knew her.

His mouth slid down her neck. His breath blew over the sensitive skin. Then she felt the press of his mouth against her. The lick of his tongue. Arousal spiked through her and she found herself arching against him.

His hands—big, strong—slid down between their bodies. His fingers curled around the small, silken strap of her belt.

Then he loosened the tie she'd made. The robe parted. She'd just put underwear on beneath the robe—her sexiest bra and panties. Black, with lace at the cups of her bra and lace around the top of her panties.

His head lifted. He stared down at her body. "The first time..." The dark rumble of his voice sent goose bumps rising over her. "It will be wild and hard because I've waited too long for you."

Wild and hard didn't sound so bad to her. It sounded exciting. Perfect.

"The second time..." Oh, but she loved the deep, dark sound of his voice. "I'll savor you."

Her hands flew back and slapped down on the table because her knees had just gone seriously weak right then. She needed to brace herself. She needed—

He lifted her into his arms. The move was so unexpected that a shocked laugh escaped her. "I can walk, Dylan."

"And I like holding you, Rachel."

But he didn't take her to the bedroom. He stopped near the couch. He lowered her down until her toes skimmed the edge of the carpet. She was glad they'd stopped there. Rachel didn't want to go into her bedroom. Jack had been there the night before. Each time she saw the bed, she thought of him.

She only wanted to think of Dylan. He'd said that this night was just about them. He was right.

Dylan pushed the robe off her shoulders. It pooled at her feet. Then his fingers slid down her arms. Slowly. Sensually.

But he'd promised her hard and wild.

"Have to taste first," he growled. He dropped to his knees before her. He was still fully dressed. "Need you… to want me…just as badly."

She did want him badly. So badly that it felt as if her body were burning from the inside.

He unhooked her bra and tossed it aside. And his mouth closed over her breast.

No tentative touches. No hesitations. He just took and she loved it. This time, when she needed balance, her hands flew to clasp his shoulders. His skin was so warm beneath her touch, and his mouth…

Her eyes closed and a moan slid past her lips.

He was licking her, kissing her and making her wild.

And his hand was pushing between her thighs. "Love these," he said as his fingers caught the edge of her panties. "Love 'em so much, I'll buy you a new pair just like them." Then he ripped the panties out of his way.

Her eyes snapped back open. "Dylan?"

He stared up at her, his eyes hot with passion. "Now, Rachel. I warned you…"

It will be wild and hard because I've waited too long for you.

He tumbled her back onto the couch cushions. Before she could even pull in a startled breath, he was there. He'd yanked open the snap of his jeans, pulled down the zipper and he pushed between her legs.

She arched up, ready—

But Dylan stopped, swearing. He fumbled in the rear pocket of his jeans and pulled out a small foil packet. In seconds, he was back with her.

She arched her hips toward him.

There was no hesitation. No slow glide.

There was only passion. Need. He drove into her and she lost her breath. He withdrew, and her nails raked down his back because she wanted him in, deeper.

Her legs locked around his hips. His fingers threaded with hers. He thrust again and again, and the tempo was just as he'd promised. Wild and hard and there was nothing but the two of them. Only the pleasure, only that moment. Only—

The world seemed to explode around her. Her body stiffened as the release hit, a surge of pleasure that swept through her, and Rachel cried out.

Dylan kept thrusting. Harder. Deeper. Thrusts that lifted up her body, that made the climax she felt last and last.

Then he tensed against her and held her tighter while he roared her name.

Being with him hadn't been awkward. It had been hot and wild and perfect.

Even better than in her dreams.

THE LIGHTS WERE still on at Rachel's place. The lights were on and the EOD agent was still skulking outside her building in the shadows, and...

The pub was getting busy.

Jack smiled as he watched a trio of drunken men fall out of the pub. They were just what he'd been waiting for.

He walked toward them, whistling. One guy was

barely steady on his feet. The fellow was trying to hail a taxi.

Jack bumped him, just a bit. A little nudge. Just hard enough to send the guy stumbling into traffic. Tires squealed. Horns honked wildly.

The guy's drunk friends grabbed for him.

A taxi missed the fellow by about two feet.

Jack was already far past the men by that point. *He'd* escaped to the shadows, certain that the drunken men hadn't seen him clearly. But the little drama was attracting new attention as people swarmed toward the man sprawled on the street.

The drama was even attracting the interest of the skulking EOD agent. And all Jack needed was for the man to be distracted for a few moments…

Jack sidled toward Dylan Foxx's car. He had a little gift to leave for Dylan.

You're out of this game. You won't touch Rachel again.

The darkness of the night could hide so much. He'd always enjoyed killing in that darkness.

Chapter Five

Rachel fought to catch her breath. She couldn't do it. Maybe it was because Dylan held her pinned to the couch or maybe it was because aftershocks of pleasure still pulsed through her body.

But she was panting and her heart was racing so fast that it shook her chest.

Dylan lifted his head and gazed down at her. "That should've taken the edge off," he said as his words seemed to rumble against her.

His voice... A shiver slid over her.

"It should've, but it didn't," he said flatly. A dark, warning edge was layered in the words. "I still want you, just as badly as before." But he was withdrawing from her, and the hard slide of his body had her gasping.

"Don't worry," Dylan said as his hands slipped from hers. "I already told you, we're just getting started."

Then he was on his feet, standing beside the couch, staring down at her. Rachel tried to reach for her robe.

He caught her hands. "Don't. I want you to stay just like that. I'll take care of you."

She stilled.

His fingers slid over the inside of her wrist, caressing the spot just above her rapidly beating pulse point.

Then he pulled away. He headed toward her bathroom. Rachel tried to suck in some deep, fortifying breaths while he was gone.

Her legs were trembling. *She* was trembling.

The floor creaked. Her head jerked up. Dylan was already back. He'd zipped and buttoned his jeans, and they hung low on his hips. He had a soft cloth in his hand. He bent and carefully pressed the cloth to the tender flesh between her thighs.

Rachel flinched. "Dylan..."

His gaze held hers. "Was I too rough?"

She shook her head.

"Good." He tossed the cloth aside. "Because this time, I get to savor."

She couldn't have spoken then even if—

A phone rang, the shrill cry loud in her apartment. She glanced to the left. It wasn't her phone.

It was his. Dylan's phone was on the end table, vibrating.

"It could be Mercer," Rachel whispered. "We should... we should get it."

His jaw locked. She knew he didn't want to move. She didn't *want* him moving anywhere.

Because she wanted to savor him, too.

The phone stopped ringing.

He smiled at her.

And the phone began its peeling cry once more.

"Don't *move*," he ordered her again.

Then he was stalking toward his phone.

She inched up a bit, staring over at him.

A frown pulled his brows low as Dylan reached for his phone. "Blocked number."

A chill swept over her skin.

Dylan swiped his finger over the screen. "Who is this?" he demanded. His finger tapped on the screen once more. A crack of static filled the room. Static then…laughter.

He'd put the call on speakerphone.

Rachel reached for her robe. She was breaking his not-moving rule. He could deal with it.

That laughter was familiar to her. It was familiar, and so was the voice that said—

"Agent Foxx, just who the hell do you *think* I am?"

Jack.

She was on her feet in an instant and rushing toward Dylan.

Dylan had turned to stone.

"Rachel knows who I am," that familiar voice continued, deep and low. "She knows me very, very well."

Dylan's gaze caught hers. "Does she? Well, guess what? Turns out I know her pretty well, too."

She froze.

"You'll never know her the way I do." Jack was smug now. "Rachel loves me. Did she tell you that? She loves me so much that even after everything that I did to her, Rachel couldn't bring herself to kill me."

Rachel fought hard not to let any expression cross her face right then.

"Rachel doesn't give a damn about you," Dylan replied, his own voice clipped. "She knows exactly what you are—a killer, and she wants to see you locked up."

"Or maybe…" Now a mocking tone had entered Jack's words. "Maybe she just wants to see me again. Maybe Rachel misses me just as much as I miss her."

She shook her head, the move instinctive.

A siren echoed outside. Rachel's gaze flashed toward

her window, then back to Dylan. She hurried to grab her phone. She needed to call the EOD. They could try and get a trace on the call. She tapped in the number for headquarters and brought the phone to her ear. When the agent answered her call, Rachel whispered, identifying herself, then she said, "Jack is on the line with Agent Foxx. The killer just called—"

"Is that my sweet Rachel?" Jack asked. "Standing there, is she? Listening to all that I have to say."

Dylan was as still as a statue.

His silence seemed to infuriate Jack. "Then why don't you both listen to this?" The words were harder now. Snapping. "You want to bring me in, Agent Foxx? You think you're the man who can finally bag the infamous Jack? Then come and get me. Just *you,* got it? You come to find me, and I'll be waiting for you behind Ford's Theatre. Right there in the alley. You and me."

Dylan didn't speak.

"Leave Rachel behind because right now…this isn't about her, is it?" Jack taunted. "It's about us. Her two lovers."

Rachel shook her head. No, Jack had never been—

"And if you aren't here in fifteen minutes, then I'll just kill the first loser who is dumb enough to cross my path. I'm feeling a little…angry tonight." But it wasn't just anger coating his words. It sounded more like fury. "First my client double-crosses me, and then I see you… spending the night with *my* girl. Things like that tend to wreck my control."

The sound of sirens filled the room again.

And…did she hear the sirens coming from Dylan's phone, too?

"Fifteen minutes," Jack snapped. "Get here or some fool will die in your place."

He hung up then.

"Did you get all of that?" Rachel asked the agent on the line because she'd turned her speakerphone on, too.

"Yes," Helen Grant said, her voice cool and in control. Rachel had worked with the other woman a few times before. "And I'll get support personnel en route. Dylan, get to Ford's Theatre. We'll have a team to back you up."

Rachel tossed her phone toward Dylan as she ran to the bedroom. It wasn't just about having another team there. She planned to be there, too. *Dylan would have backup all right—me.*

She grabbed for her clothes, dressing as quickly as she could. She ran back into the den seconds later.

And saw that Thomas was coming into her apartment. Dylan was at the door, heading out.

He's leaving me?

"Stay here," Dylan directed her as he glanced over his shoulder. "This will be over soon."

He was crazy. "Not happening." She marched toward him. "I think you've got me confused with a civilian— and not an EOD agent."

His dark eyes glittered down at her. "I don't have time to argue. Please…just stay here."

Then he was just—gone. What the hell?

Thomas shrugged and lifted his hands. "My orders are to watch you."

"And my orders are to bring down Jack. Not just sit here while Dylan risks *his* life." Because that wasn't the definition of a team.

One person facing the danger?

One person being safe?

No way.

She rushed out right after Dylan. Thomas tried to stop her, but she just yanked free of his hold. Her feet thudded down the stairs, and she caught up with Dylan just as he was heading for the door of her building. "It's a trap!" She grabbed his arm.

He swung around to face her. "You think I don't know that? Why do you think I want you to stay here with Thomas?"

"So you can face all the danger yourself." She shook her head. "Teammates take the risk together." And Jack—he was her problem. It was personal for her. Not just about the EOD. Not just about stopping a killer.

"I don't have time—"

She sprinted ahead of him and into the night. "Then catch up."

Dylan's car waited in the parking spot just a few feet away. She ran toward it.

RACHEL EXITED THE BUILDING, running ahead of Dylan Foxx.

Jack stiffened.

Rachel had *heard* his orders. So had Dylan. Dylan was to come to that meeting alone.

He's not alone.

As Jack watched, Dylan unlocked his car. He was standing at the passenger side, right next to Rachel. They were arguing.

But Rachel got in the car.

She got in the car.

Dylan ran around the vehicle and jumped into the driver's seat.

Rachel was in the car.

No. She had to get out.

Jack rushed forward. Horns blared as he ran right across the busy street.

"SO MUCH FOR listening to your senior officer," Dylan snapped. Rachel was already buckled up, and the woman's delicate jaw had locked. No matter what he said, Rachel wasn't backing down.

"Drive, Dylan. *Now.*"

Car horns honked, blaring loudly. There was a police cruiser a few feet away. The uniforms were talking with a few college-aged guys.

And...

Someone was rushing across the street.

That was why the cars were honking.

Dylan turned the ignition, frowning.

"Rachel!" It was a man's scream. The man running across the street. *"Get. Out!"*

The car's engine sputtered. The vehicle was in top condition—always perfectly maintained because it belonged to the EOD. It shouldn't have sputtered.

I know what that sputter means.

And he knew who the man was—the man shouting because he was so afraid.

"Get out!" Dylan yelled as fear froze his own blood. Not fear for him, but for Rachel. Her fingers were fumbling with the seat belt. He jerked the belt free. She opened her door. He shoved her toward the sidewalk. *"Run!"*

Then Dylan pushed open his door. He lunged out—

The car exploded.

Dylan felt a wave of fire rush over his skin, and then

he was flying, hurtling through the air as the force of the blast picked him up and tossed him ten feet.

He landed in the middle of the street. The pavement tore off the skin on his lower arms. He rolled, tumbling, and car lights blinded him as the vehicles screeched to a stop near him.

The thunder of the explosion slowly faded. Dylan shoved up to his feet. He had only one thought then— only one person mattered.

"Rachel!"

He spun back toward the car.

And saw nothing but a wall of flames.

RACHEL LAY ON the ground like a broken doll.

Her hair was spread beneath her. Her arms limp.

Jack crouched over her. Others were running toward them now. His fingers slid to her throat. Felt for her pulse.

Alive.

Jack exhaled slowly. "You shouldn't have been in the car with him." This was all Dylan's fault.

"Rachel!"

Jack jerked at the bellow. His head snapped up and his eyes narrowed. So Dylan had survived, too.

Unfortunate.

But Dylan was on the other side of those flames. Dylan couldn't see him. Not yet.

It had been so long since he'd touched Rachel. Jack's fingers slid over her throat.

Her eyes fluttered, then cracked open. It was dark, and the flames were behind him. He wasn't sure that she could see his face.

Even if she did, would she recognize him?

Doubtful. He slowly slid back. Bodies bumped into him. People who were eager to help Rachel.

And the EOD agent was fighting to get to her side.

He backed up a bit more and took off his baseball cap. It would be easier to just blend in with the crowd.

He was good at blending in.

Dylan Foxx rushed by him, so close that their shoulders collided.

Dylan didn't even spare him a second glance. The man was too consumed, too focused on Rachel.

Anger churned within Jack. *She isn't yours, Agent Foxx. She never will be.*

RACHEL OPENED HER EYES and saw a swirl of faces above her. And just behind them, flames shot into the sky.

She was pretty sure those flames had been a car a few moments before.

"Dylan!" She shoved to her feet and pushed through the crowd that had gathered. Where was he? Where—

Hard hands caught her and yanked her tightly against a strong, muscled body. The scent of smoke clung to Dylan as he held her in a grip that crushed her. "I was afraid you wouldn't get out," he whispered. His mouth was close to her neck, his breath rushing over her skin.

She held him just as fiercely. They'd both nearly died in that car. "He did it." Jack. He'd set Dylan up to die.

Only… *You came back to warn me.* He'd wanted her out of the car, and he'd rushed toward them just before the vehicle exploded.

If Jack had been at the scene then… Rachel pushed against Dylan. "He's still here." Her gaze scanned the crowd of onlookers. Some were staring at the flames with wide eyes. Some were even snapping pictures on their phones.

"He had on a baseball cap," she whispered. That part she remembered.

And she remembered the sound of his bellowing cry. *Rachel! Get out!*

He'd been ready to watch Dylan die, but he hadn't been ready to let her go.

Fury churned within her. She turned so that her back bumped into Dylan's chest. There was one man close by who wore a baseball cap. He was snapping a picture of the flames. But he was too small to be Jack. He appeared to be barely five foot seven, and Jack—he was well over six feet.

Where are you?

"Rachel! Dylan!" Thomas pushed through the crowd. His gaze flew over them. "You need medics."

She didn't. Okay, her head had slammed into the concrete pretty hard when the blast had knocked her down, but she was fine. Rachel looked over at Dylan. Her breath expelled on a hard rush when she saw the dark splotches on his clothes. *Blood.* She'd been so happy to see him before that she hadn't even realized he was hurt.

But Dylan shook his head. "We search the crowd. Now. He's here."

Cops were there. EMTs. A fire truck raced toward them.

"It was a bomb," Dylan said, jaw hardening. "Set to go when I turned the ignition."

She didn't want to think about how close she'd just

come to losing Dylan. Despite the heat from the flames, Rachel's skin felt chilled.

She straightened her shoulders. "I'll find him." She took a step forward.

The world seemed to grow darker then. Was the smoke thickening? Her head throbbed, and her knees gave way.

Rachel would have slammed right into the ground again but strong hands caught her. She was lifted up, held tightly and a voice said, "I've got you."

That wasn't Dylan's voice. Dylan didn't have a faint Irish brogue.

She looked into Aidan's eyes. Aidan looked stunned. Scared. His eyes were wide as he tried to settle her on her feet again.

Only her legs didn't quite seem to be working the way they should.

"I heard the explosion. It reminded me…back in Ireland, there were so many attacks when I was a boy," Aidan told her, pain echoing in his voice. His beard was gone and his face seemed to reflect the terror he felt.

Dizziness rushed through Rachel before she could respond to him. Her body swayed. This time Dylan was the one to steady her. "Rachel? Baby, what is it?"

Then Dylan's fingers were sliding through her hair, and she jerked when he touched the spot that hurt and throbbed the worst. "Concussion," he said. "Damn it, Rachel, you should've told me!"

It was a bump on the head. Nothing more. So small. She'd walked away from plenty worse.

But her legs weren't walking now. And even though Rachel tried to talk to Dylan, she couldn't.

Because the darkness claimed her once more.

"I'M LEAVING," RACHEL SAID, her voice absolutely certain. She'd been in that hospital room for twenty-four hours—*twenty-four!*—and she was going stir-crazy.

A concussion. The doctors had been so worried because she'd passed out. Twice. They'd insisted that she stay put for observation.

She'd argued.

Dylan had told her to save her protests because she wasn't going anywhere. Then Mercer had gotten involved, and Rachel found herself benched for twenty-four sickeningly boring hours.

But no more. She was dressed, and she was ready to bust out of that place.

Dylan stared at her. His wounds had been bandaged. She could see the edge of white tape around his arms. They'd both been so lucky. If they hadn't moved fast enough—*no*. She slammed the door shut on that particular train of thought. She was not going there. She didn't want to think of all the *what-ifs* that could have been.

Focus on the fact that you're both safe.

She was also focusing on the fact that Dylan was finally back with her. After he'd gotten Mercer involved and they'd secured her at the hospital, Dylan had vanished.

"You're the only reason I'm alive," Dylan said as he came closer to her.

She rubbed her hands over her jeans-clad thighs. She'd already dressed because there was no way she was staying in that hospital any longer.

"How did he get access to the car?" Rachel asked. That had been worrying her.

"Thomas said there was a commotion last night and that he stepped away from guard duty for a few moments." Dylan's head inclined. "That's when Jack must've set the bomb. Then he called me and lured me out."

She paced toward him. Put her hand on his chest. "He doesn't…he doesn't usually go for attacks like that." He'd always used a gun or a knife before. Up-close-and-personal kills.

Dylan's lips twisted. "Guess I warranted special circumstances."

Or she had. Her gaze searched his. "He wants you out of the way. He's going to attack again."

Dylan's eyes held hers. "And he wants you alive."

She was still trying to wrap her head around that. Jack had actually rushed to save her. Noelle was right. "I was so sure he wanted me dead."

"I think we both know he wants a lot more than death from you." He turned away. "But he's not getting it."

She followed him. The doctors had tried to tell her that she needed to be taken out in a wheelchair. She'd just glared back at them. The last thing she wanted was any extra attention being drawn to her. She'd go out just fine on her own two feet.

Dylan was at her side as they walked through the hospital corridor. A few nurses gave him long, lingering looks.

It was the bad-boy appeal at play again, she knew it.

Outside, Thomas was waiting near his SUV. When he saw her, he hurried forward. "I'm so sorry, Rachel." Emotion was there, *real* emotion, shining in his golden eyes. "This attack is on me."

She shook her head. "No, it's on Jack." Thomas hadn't planted the bomb. "And I'm guessing there are no new leads on him?"

They climbed into the vehicle. Thomas was in the front. She and Dylan were in the back.

"No, no new leads." Thomas sounded grim. Disgusted.

She felt the same way. "We know he's watching us."

"He's watching *you*," Dylan corrected. He wasn't touching her. Odd. He actually *hadn't* touched her, not since she'd gone to the hospital.

Maybe because he'd realized that wanting her could prove fatal?

Rachel swallowed the lump in her throat. Dylan had agreed to play the charade of lovers, but that had been before he came within seconds of dying in an explosion.

"Three years," Rachel said, her brows furrowing. "That's a long time for him to vanish from my life."

"Who says that he has been gone that whole time?" This question came from Thomas as he steered them through the streets of D.C. "It could be that he was close by…and you only realized it now because he decided to *make* you aware of him."

She'd had plenty of time to think in that hospital room. A guard had been at her door and Dylan—he'd been gone. He'd left her, heading back to the mission. Rachel knew the drill. The mission always came first. So she shouldn't have been hurt.

But she had been.

"If he wants me," she said, clearing her throat because she had a plan now, "then he can get me."

Dylan's head jerked toward her. His eyes looked like black fire. He gritted out, "The hell he can."

But she nodded. "Jack proved that he doesn't want me dead. We need to give him a chance to get close to me again. If he takes me—" the way he'd abducted her three years ago "—then you can track him."

Every EOD agent had a small tracking device implanted beneath the skin. In case the agent was captured or in case the agent got lost in enemy territory, Mercer wanted a safety system in place for retrieving that agent.

Dr. Tina Jamison had put a new chip in for Rachel just a few months before. If Jack took her...*then we've got you.*

It was dark outside. So Rachel couldn't see Dylan's face clearly as he said, "That's not an option." No, she couldn't see him, but she could hear the crack of fury in his words.

Thomas kept driving.

Dylan wasn't being logical. "We can't just let Jack run loose around the city. We don't know when he'll attack again." And if Jack was using bombs now...talk about a whole new nightmare. Civilians could get caught in the flames. They'd been lucky that no one else had been injured when Dylan's car exploded.

"We don't know when, but we do know *who* he's going after."

Her heart squeezed at his words. "I don't get to be the bait, but you do? That's the plan?"

"That was always the plan. You know that." His head turned away from her, and he gazed out the window. "I just need to make myself a target—"

She grabbed his arm. He might not be touching her, but she needed to touch him. "How many times do you think you can cheat death?"

He didn't look at her. Whatever he saw out that window had to be fascinating.

"Dylan!"

"As many as it takes."

The vehicle slowed. They pulled toward a parking garage. A familiar one. They were headed to the main EOD office.

She sat in silence as they passed through the security checkpoint. Then they were in the cavernous garage. Dylan held the door for her when she climbed from the SUV.

"Thomas..." Rachel glanced his way. "We'll catch up with you inside."

Thomas hesitated. "Mercer's waiting."

Right. The big, fierce boss. But it was *her* life. "Let him wait. I need to speak with Dylan. Alone." Because they needed to clear the air between them before anything else happened.

Thomas's gaze assessed first her, then Dylan. He nodded. "Good luck," he murmured to Dylan then Thomas headed for the elevator.

Rachel didn't move. She wasn't exactly sure where to start this little scene.

Dylan exhaled. "Say it, Rachel."

Fine. So maybe she did know exactly where to start. "I close my eyes, and I picture you burning in that car."

His jaw hardened. "And I close my eyes—and you're in that damn car, burning right next to me." He turned from her, yanking a hand through his hair. "That's why this ends. I'm the bait. Hell, yes, I will be. Gladly. But I won't risk you."

"It's all about me!" Jack would never even be coming after Dylan if it weren't for her. Didn't he see that?

"I'm the senior member of this team." His voice was hard. "I make the calls." He glanced toward the elevator. Thomas was gone. Dylan rubbed his jaw. "And when we go in that building, you should know that…I'm recommending you be relocated until Jack is contained."

What?

He nodded, still not looking at her as he said, "It's the best solution."

"No, it's a ridiculous solution." She marched toward him. Caught his arm in her grip and forced him to look at her. "And pulling rank on me?" Rachel shook her head. "Bad form, Dylan. Bad."

His eyes narrowed.

But she wasn't done. Not even close. "You're the leader. Good for you. Normally, you say jump, and every member of your team leaps. Not this time, though, because I'm not just part of your team." She took a deep breath. "Now I'm your lover."

"I'm damn well aware of just what you are to me," he growled.

"Then you know that you can't just push me aside—"

"I know that when you're close, I'm at risk."

His words shocked her, and Rachel let him go.

"I can't think clearly when you're with me. My control…it *shreds.*"

"You wanted us to be together…"

He nodded, but said, "And I knew that when we crossed that line, things would change."

She didn't like the tone of his voice. Too hard. Too rough. "You…you don't want—"

"I want you too much, that's the problem." And he stepped back. Again, putting more distance between them. Did he have any idea how much that hurt her? "I need to keep my head clear. I rushed out of your apartment last night, not thinking. I *should've* checked my surroundings. As soon as the engine sputtered—I should've known what was happening. But I was too focused on you."

"I was just as focused on you," she whispered back because he'd given her so much pleasure. Her body had been humming. She'd been so attuned to him.

Then, in an instant, everything had changed.

"I can't afford that weakness, not now." His words seemed to snap out.

Rachel's brows lowered. Had he just called her a weakness?

"I've got Jack's attention. Obviously, I've got it. And that was the plan all along."

She didn't like the direction this little chat was taking.

"So now I move forward." His tone was that of a commander, not a lover. "And you...you, Rachel, you're going to have to stay the hell back."

She actually did stumble back a step then.

"You don't have a choice," he continued. She couldn't read past the mask he wore. "I'm in charge of this mission, and you have to follow the orders I give."

Pulling rank. Again.

She didn't even know who he was right then. This sure wasn't the Dylan she knew. Pain twisted within her. "Yes, sir." Her own words were cold. This *wasn't* the way it should be between them.

She turned from him. So much for clearing the air. Dylan had his own agenda. She took another step then stopped. "Why didn't you come to see me in the hospital?"

When she'd been hurt a few months back, he'd stayed at her side the entire time. But this time...

"Because I had a mission."

Her shoulders straightened. That was the response of

an agent, but they were supposed to be *more* than just teammates. Something was changing with Dylan. This single-minded focus that he had. Almost an obsession with catching Jack.

It…scared her.

She'd thought that she knew Dylan. She'd trusted him enough to take him as a lover.

But I thought that I knew Jack, too.

She didn't look back at him again. She was too worried about what she might see.

Chapter Six

"Jack took the bait," Mercer said as he leaned back in his chair. A faint smile was on his face. "Obviously."

Obviously? Dylan stood a few feet from Mercer. He hadn't bothered to sit down. Rachel and Thomas were both seated, and Noelle stood near the back wall. *The better to watch us all.* But that was what the profiler did. She watched and she judged everyone else.

"We tapped into the traffic cameras near Rachel's place. Tried to get an image of Jack from that night." Mercer tapped his fingers on the desk. "But Jack was careful. He kept his ball cap on, and he made sure that we only saw his back."

Figured.

"He'll make contact again," Noelle said.

"You mean when he tries to kill me again?" Dylan answered back. Yeah, he was more than ready for that *contact* to come. Only this time, he'd make sure Rachel wasn't anywhere around when Jack got close.

"Killing you does seem to be the current goal," Noelle murmured.

Dylan grunted. He'd figured that out when his ride became a ball of fire. "Are we a go on the transfer?" he asked Mercer. He'd spent the past twenty-four hours pushing for this change. Mercer hadn't been on board, not at first. Dylan had worked hard and convinced the man to see things his way.

From the corner of his eye, Dylan saw Rachel tense. *I'm sorry, Rachel, but I'm benching you.*

She wouldn't like it. But she'd be safe. Dylan knew that if he didn't get Rachel out of there, she *would* be at his side when Jack came again. Only she might not walk away with a bump on the head. She might not walk away at all.

That wasn't a risk he was willing to take.

"The transfer is set," Mercer said slowly as his gaze drifted to Rachel. "And the doctors agreed with your assessment."

Rachel's fingers tightened around the armrests. "What's going on?"

Mercer's fingers stopped tapping. "You came back to work too quickly after your last attack. Those stab wounds were severe, Agent Mancini. And now, in light of the concussion you just suffered, it's clear that you shouldn't be back in the field just yet."

She immediately surged to her feet. "No, Mercer, you can't—"

"You suffered a vicious attack a few months ago, Rachel, when the rogue agent—"

"I know exactly what the rogue agent did to me." Rachel cut off Mercer.

The EOD director raised an eyebrow.

"After all, I was there," Rachel continued, body tight. "I was there, fighting, when he stabbed me again and again. I was there when he rushed away, and I could only lie there, bleeding out on my apartment floor. I. Was. There."

Dylan's hands had fisted.

"I was the one in the hospital, hooked to machines. So believe me, I know just how vicious the attack was." She huffed out a breath. "And I know I survived. I'm back here, ready to work—"

"But you collapsed last night," Mercer told her. His voice was soft, mild, and Dylan actually saw a hint of sympathy in the man's normally cold gaze.

"A small bump on the head." She waved it away. "I didn't—"

"If you'd been fully recovered, you might not have needed a civilian to pick you up from the street." Now the sympathy was gone from Mercer's voice.

"But I—"

"Dylan was right. You're not ready."

Oh, hell.

Rachel's head swiveled toward him. Her gaze—shocked, hurt—held his. "Dylan? You think I'm not *ready* for this?"

"Um, Agent Foxx is the one who told me that you needed to be transferred to desk duty for a few more weeks. Under the circumstances, I do think it's for the best."

Rachel shook her head.

Thomas glanced at Dylan, his gaze knowing.

Yes, I'm trying to protect her. I'll do anything to keep her safe.

Even, as Rachel had said, *pull rank.*

Even hurt her. Because Dylan could tell Rachel was hurt. And furious.

Noelle shifted slightly, moving from her left foot to her right.

Dylan didn't move at all. He couldn't. Not with Rachel's stark gaze on him.

"Don't worry," Mercer told Rachel. "You know Agent Foxx can handle this case. He's been after Jack since long before you even joined the EOD. He'll do what is necessary to bring the killer in, you can count on that."

Rachel flinched. "What is necessary?"

No, oh, no, she'd better not be thinking—

"I think he already has," Rachel murmured. Then she shook her head and faced Mercer once more. Her chin was up, her shoulders straight. "I want you to reconsider." Just like that, the emotion was gone from her voice. She'd soldier on. That was Rachel. Always so strong. "I *know* Jack. I can—"

"Jack has taken the bait that Dylan provided. We're confident that he will be apprehended soon." Mercer was obviously finished with that discussion. "My assistant, Judith, will give you new orders, Agent Mancini."

Rachel stiffened.

"But…" Again, a hint of sympathy flashed in Mercer's eyes. "Perhaps you'd rather just take a few days off before starting your new assignment? You've been through quite a lot lately."

She glanced down at her hands. "I joined the EOD because I wanted to make a difference in this world."

"You have," Mercer assured her. "But this particular case is over for you." He straightened in his chair. "You're dismissed now, Agent."

"Yes," Rachel murmured. "I guess I am." She turned and headed for the door. She didn't glance over at Dylan even though—damn it—he *wanted* her to look at him again.

She walked slowly. She kept her head up the whole way. Not bowed. Proud.

The door closed behind her.

Thomas exhaled slowly. "You didn't ask for it, but I'm telling you all…that was the wrong move. That woman *deserves* to be on this case, she—"

"Jack isn't going to hurt her." Noelle advanced and took the chair that Rachel had vacated. "She won't be his next target. He's clearly shown us that he will protect her." Her gaze cut to Dylan. "And he'll eliminate the man who he views as taking Rachel from him."

"You think you know the killers, don't you?" A hard edge entered Thomas's voice. "But what happens if you're wrong? What if we don't always act just like you think?"

We?

Dylan glanced toward Mercer and found that the EOD director was staring straight at him.

"Right about now," Mercer murmured, "Rachel is discovering just what her desk duty entails."

It wasn't just about being pulled off the case. It was about Rachel being temporarily relocated to the EOD's smaller facility in Atlanta.

She'd be safer there. Out of Jack's sight.

"Are you quite certain," Mercer asked Dylan quietly, "that move was the best one? Rachel Mancini isn't the type of woman to cower in the corner when danger looms."

No, she wasn't. She was the type of woman who would risk her life. *For me.* Just like she'd put herself at risk when she rushed out of her apartment and insisted on coming with him to that meeting with Jack. She'd been so worried he was in danger.

She hadn't thought about the risk to herself.

"It's the only move that I have," Dylan said.

Mercer inclined his head. "Then I hope you don't live to regret it."

RACHEL FELT AS if she were about to explode. Just breathing was an effort, and the pain—*the betrayal*—twisting inside her was like a red-hot poker in her stomach.

She waited in Dylan's office. She knew he had to show up there as soon as he was finished with Mercer. A meeting that no longer included her since Dylan had had her removed from the case.

While I was stuck in the hospital. Now she knew exactly why he hadn't stayed with her at the hospital. He'd been busy working to get her sent down to Atlanta.

The door opened with a squeak. Rachel was in Dylan's chair. She pushed with her feet, making the chair roll so that she faced the door. And him.

I gave myself to you, Dylan. Why did you do this to me? Why?

He stared at her a moment. Then he stepped fully into the small office and shut the door behind him. "I guess you'll be heading out soon. Your flight—"

"Is tomorrow," Rachel managed to say in an almost normal voice. "Yes, that's what I've been told." She would not lose control in front of him. But she would get to the bottom of the mystery that was Dylan. Something that Mercer said kept nagging at her. "Thanks to you, of course."

He crossed his arms over his chest. "EOD agents get transferred to new assignments all the time. It's part of life here, you know that."

Seriously? He was trying to play that card?

They were alone. No eyes on them. No ears. So she said *exactly* what she was thinking. "We had sex, Dylan. It was supposed to mean something." It had sure meant something to her.

He glanced away from her. "There's us, Rachel, and then there's the EOD. The missions we have to take... We both knew that when we crossed that particular line—"

"The line that made us lovers?"

"We wouldn't be able to stay in the field together."

Her breath caught. "You...told Mercer?"

"No."

That was something.

"But the transfer was going to happen, no matter what."

She wanted to shake him. This wasn't the Dylan she knew. Rachel jumped to her feet. *"Stop it!"*

He blinked at her.

"What is going on with you? I thought... We work together, Dylan. You and I. There's no one closer to me than you. There's no one I trust like I do you." But that trust was shaking. He'd requested she be sent away, even knowing how important this particular case was to her.

He didn't respond. Damn him.

"Why are you on this case?" And it was back again, the twisting suspicion that Mercer had planted with his words.

He's been after Jack since long before you even joined the EOD. He'll do what is necessary to bring the killer in, you can count on that.

"I'm after him because the EOD wants the threat Jack poses to be eliminated."

That answer sounded rehearsed. Like he was just

spewing some line he'd been taught before. "When I first met you…you were hunting Jack then."

His gaze slid back to hers.

She struggled to put the pieces of this puzzle together. She'd read all of the case files on Jack and she knew… "You'd been hunting him for six months before that. I remember reading it in the reports."

He nodded. "So you know that I won't stop until I—"

"Why were you the agent in charge back then? How'd you get landed with Jack's case?"

He pushed back his shoulders. "Mercer assigned me to the case."

Rachel had worked intimately with Dylan on so many cases, and because of that she knew him very well. She also knew all of his "tells"—the signs that he gave when he twisted the truth. Or when he just flat-out lied.

That shoulder rollback? He did it right before he lied.

"That's not true." Her head was aching again, but there was no way she was about to let that weakness show. "You…you requested to be on the assignment, didn't you?" That was a pure hunch on her part.

But after a tense moment, Dylan nodded.

"Why?"

"Because he's a dangerous man. Jack needs to be—"

"Stop it! Just tell me the truth." She was almost begging him. And Rachel was so confused. Lost and confused because she'd thought they always had honesty between them.

Now she wasn't sure what was happening or if they had anything between them. She exhaled slowly. "Why were you after him?"

His lips thinned. "Because he killed someone I knew."

"Knew?" Rachel pressed. But she suddenly realized

that maybe she didn't want to hear this part. Because that poker was back in her gut, burning hotter than before.

"Shannon Morgan. She was his fourth victim. Shannon and I were...close."

It hurt. So much that she retreated a step. "You were lovers."

A grim nod was her answer.

He'd had lovers. Of course he had. She'd thought... just the other night...Rachel shook her head. "There's more to this story."

More that she just didn't know.

He glanced down at the floor. "We talked about getting married."

She grabbed the edge of the desk. *He'd loved Shannon.* "Why didn't you tell me?"

He shook his head.

"Dylan—"

"Because they were together!" The words burst from him. Angry. Snarling.

Her hold on the desk tightened.

"Shannon and I...we talked about a future together. She knew what I wanted but she wasn't ready to settle down. She met Jack. He seduced her, charmed her. She thought the guy actually cared about her."

A dull ringing seemed to sound in her ears. "But he was just getting close to her because she was an assignment. The same way he got close to me."

"She told me that she wanted to be with him. Her 'Jack.' She broke up with me. She went to be with him. And the next day, she was dead. He'd put a bullet in her heart and left his calling card in her hand."

There was grief in his voice. Grief and fury.

Rachel realized where she fit into his equation then. "It was always personal for you. You wanted vengeance."

"I wanted *justice*."

She didn't believe him. "You...you used me." She'd never thought that someone else had been involved. When they were together...he'd said that it was just about her. About him.

But as soon as they'd realized that Jack was back in town, Dylan had been the one to push. He'd wanted them to play at being lovers, then to take it a step further... to *be* lovers.

"That's why three years passed and you never so much as tried to kiss me." She'd been blind. *Trusting the wrong man, again.*

"You don't know what you're talking about." He raked a hand over his face. "You're tired. You need to rest before your flight."

A flight she wasn't taking.

"You got close to me because that made you close to Jack. You wanted his attention." Judging by that bomb blast... "You got it."

Dylan stalked toward the door. "I'll get Thomas to take you back to your place. He's going to have guard duty until your flight leaves tomorrow—"

"Do you still love her?" She hadn't meant to ask, but the question whispered from her.

She saw his shoulders stiffen.

"This isn't just about Shannon," Dylan told her.

"No," she agreed, sad now. Because she grieved for what could have been. "Because she's gone, and I'm right here. Only you can't even look at me." That was fine. She wasn't sure that she wanted to look at him right then. "Don't worry about calling Thomas. I can find my own way out of here."

He turned toward her. Rachel tried to shove past him.

He caught her and held her in a tight grip. She twisted her wrist. She'd break free easily enough. He wasn't dealing with some—

"Don't." The word broke from him. Pain. Fury. Grief.

So much emotion, but Rachel didn't think it was for her. It was for a woman long dead.

She'd read the file on Shannon Morgan. Shannon had been working at the Pentagon when she was killed. A woman with a bright future, plenty of friends…

The report never mentioned Dylan. Why? Because he'd been EOD? Had Mercer made sure that Dylan's name stayed out of that nice, neat report?

"You know I wanted you." His hold tightened on her. "You know I *still* want you."

But he'd managed to keep that desire in check easily enough. Until he'd needed them to be lovers.

Now she knew why he'd reacted so strongly when she'd told him that she and Jack hadn't been lovers.

Jack and Shannon had been.

"I thought I was so careful." She wouldn't let him see how much she hurt then. "But I guess we all make mistakes." She just kept putting her trust in the wrong men.

"You didn't make a mistake with me."

He should try explaining that to the heart that felt as if it were breaking.

"When this is over," Dylan said, giving a hard nod, "we'll move forward. We can see where this relationship goes—"

She laughed then. The sound was bitter. Hollow.

Then she pulled her hand from his. "It's not going

anywhere. We are over, Dylan. No more being on a team. No more being lovers."

He swallowed. "You're angry. I get that—"

"No, you don't. I thought you actually knew me, but I was so wrong about that. If you really knew me, you'd realize that *angry* doesn't come close to how I feel." There was too much pain for her to even touch the anger yet. "You're looking for justice for a woman who's dead. I wanted justice for myself." Justice, not revenge. "And you took that away from me." All of her training. All of her work. "You took it all from me."

Then, because she would *not* break in front of him, Rachel headed for the door. With one foot in front of the other, she walked down the hallway. She went straight to Mercer's office.

Mercer's assistant, Judith, rose when Rachel approached. Judith's pretty features slackened with worry. "Rachel, what's wrong?"

Rachel just shook her head. "I have to see him."

Judith was normally Mercer's guard dog. If you didn't have an appointment, she didn't let you pass into his sanctum.

But Judith was also Rachel's friend. She opened Mercer's door.

Rachel slipped inside. Mercer glanced up, his face reflecting a flash of surprise. "Agent Mancini, what—"

"I'm done, Mercer." She'd put three years of blood and sweat into the EOD. In return, she'd been shoved aside.

His eyelids flickered. "No, surely, you—"

"I'm out." There wasn't more for her to say. She wasn't going to Atlanta. Wasn't going to wait quietly down there and then get transferred back up to D.C. when Dylan thought it was safe enough for her to return.

She'd faced danger day-in and day-out. She'd risked her life time and time again.

No more.

"I deserve a life." Not a lover who'd turn his back on her.

Then she gave one final nod to Mercer—and left.

DYLAN STARED DOWN at his clenched hands.

He'd hurt Rachel.

He'd wanted to protect her. To get her away from Jack.

She looked at me as if she didn't know who I was. As if I was some kind of damn stranger...and not her lover.

Being with her...she'd overwhelmed him, driven him to the brink of sanity. The pleasure had been unlike anything he'd ever felt before.

He wanted her. Again and again and again.

And he'd almost gotten her killed.

He was the senior agent. He should have forced Rachel to stay in her apartment. But because it was her, because he couldn't say no to her, he'd let her come with him. He'd been weak.

She'd almost been dead.

The phone on his desk rang, and he picked it up, his movements jerky. "Agent Foxx."

"My office. Now." He heard Mercer's familiar snarl, then the call ended.

Dylan didn't want to go into Mercer's office. He wanted to find Rachel. To try and explain to her—

I want to stop Jack so that you'll be safe. So that he won't ever come near you again.

That explanation wasn't good enough. She'd learned about his secrets. He knew that he should have told her before, but Jack was still an open wound for her. He just hadn't wanted to hurt her any more.

But I did.

He'd never seen quite that look in Rachel's eyes before.

He put down the phone and returned to Mercer's office. Rachel was still in the building. He'd talk with Mercer and then he'd find her. There was plenty more to say between them.

He passed Judith's desk. The woman's glare seemed to burn his skin. Dylan paused. "Judith?"

"I always knew you weren't good enough for her."

His eyes widened. *You're right. I'm not. Not even close.*

Judith pointed to Mercer's door. "He's waiting."

He fumbled and opened the door. Mercer wasn't at his desk. He was staring out the window. His hands were behind his back. His shoulders bowed.

"Shut the door," Mercer ordered without looking back.

Dylan shut the door.

Mercer exhaled. "I'm going to ask you a few questions, son, and I need you to reply honestly, you understand?"

"Yes." *No.*

"What's the most important thing in your life?"

Rachel. He cleared his throat, pushed back his shoulders and said, "The EOD."

Mercer looked back at him. "I don't know if you heard me, but I said you needed to reply *honestly.* The door's shut, and this conversation will never leave this room." Mercer arched a brow. "So let's cut the bull and try that one again. Agent Foxx, what is the most important thing in your life?"

"Rachel." Her name was torn from him.

Mercer nodded. "Better. Much better." He studied Dylan in silence for a time, then said, "But if she matters so much, then why did you push her away?"

"I'm *protecting* her."

"She's a marine. The woman can protect herself."

Dylan took a step toward his boss. "The rogue stabbed her just a few months ago. She got a concussion in Jack's blast. She's not ready to be in the field. Your own doctors said—"

"No one but you said she needed to be shipped down to Atlanta. That was totally your call as the team leader." Mercer's shoulders sagged a bit. "Don't think I don't get where you're coming from. You care about someone, and you want to keep her safe. But Rachel Mancini isn't the type of woman who will tolerate being locked up."

He wasn't locking her up. He was just trying to get her out of Jack's path. Because Jack would come gunning for Dylan again. He knew it. Rachel couldn't get caught between them.

"You think I haven't been there?" Mercer asked, surprising Dylan. "You think I don't know what it's like to care and to want to do anything and everything in your power to protect those closest to you?" Mercer's hands dropped to his sides. "We want to control everything, but sometimes we just can't."

He didn't want to control Rachel. He wanted to keep her alive.

"She's been on dozens of missions with you. You never hesitated with her before," Mercer charged.

This was different.

"Why?" his boss pressed. "Why the change now?"

Because he'd crossed a line with her. There was no way he could just look at Rachel as an operative any longer. "I put a target on my back. We both know it. I don't want Rachel getting hurt because of me."

"You mean...because of your desire to take down Jack."

Mercer always saw too much.

"I haven't forgotten about Shannon," Mercer said. "I remember all too well. You walked through that door—" he nodded toward said door "—and demanded to be lead on the investigation. Your eyes burned with fury, but your voice shook with pain." His lips twisted. "You've changed a lot in the years since then, but that fury—it's still in your eyes any time you talk about Jack. Fury like that can make a man reckless. Are you reckless, Foxx?"

"No."

"Maybe you're lying to yourself now."

He didn't understand the point of this meeting. "Look, Mercer, the heart-to-heart is not really working so much, and I need to get Rachel home—"

"No, you don't."

Something about Mercer's tone put Dylan on edge.

"Actually, she's not your concern at all any longer."

"Just because I won't be the team leader for her doesn't mean that she's not—" *Mine.* He stopped, keeping that bit back.

"Rachel Mancini is no longer a part of the EOD."

"What?"

"She resigned about ten minutes ago. I imagine she's already left the building."

"You just let her walk away? With Jack loose out there?" Dylan spun for the door.

"We both know Jack doesn't want her dead."

"No, he just wants her." *But he can't have her.* Dylan grabbed for the doorknob.

"You want her, too, and *that's* your problem, Agent. You're not thinking the way you should. Instead of using a strong, talented agent, you're letting your fury guide you." Intensity thickened in Mercer's voice. "Rachel isn't Shannon, and you need to remember that."

Dylan yanked open the door and rushed outside.

Judith's hot glare singed him.

He didn't stop to talk. He searched the whole floor, looking for Rachel.

She wasn't there.

He rounded the corner, heart racing, and nearly collided with Thomas. The man moved so silently that Dylan hadn't heard his approach.

"Where is she?" Dylan growled.

Thomas frowned at him. "Rachel? I thought she was in your office."

No, she wasn't. More searching showed that Rachel wasn't in the building at all. A security check told them that Rachel had left about five minutes before. She'd just walked away.

And left Dylan behind.

Chapter Seven

Even at night, Rachel could see the scars left by the explosion. The pavement and the nearby building were dark, seemingly lined by a thick shadow.

But she knew the darkness wasn't a shadow. Scorch marks. The blackness left behind after the explosion.

She stared down at the sidewalk. A new streetlamp was close by. The city workers were fast, she'd give them that. The streetlamp illuminated the sidewalk in the exact spot Rachel had hit when she'd been thrown by the blast.

Violence could change so much.

Voices rose in the air. Laughter. She glanced over, following those sounds to the pub. It was a busy night there. She found herself walking toward the pub, toward the light and warmth that it promised.

The pub's main door swung open beneath her hand. The place didn't remind her of death and destruction. There was laughter there. Men and women flirting.

Living.

She made her way to the bar and recognized Aidan right away as he pushed drinks across to thirsty customers. He was laughing. Despite the fear he'd shown the previous night, the man now looked as if he didn't have a care in the world.

If only she could feel that way.

Rachel eased through the crowd. Someone bumped her shoulder and she turned instinctively—and found herself staring at the blond male she'd met just a few nights before.

"Hi, there." He flashed her a wide smile. "I don't think we've met."

Seriously? Rachel actually found herself laughing in response to that. "We have," she told him, shaking her head. "You tried to buy me a drink at this very pub, and I thanked you, but didn't accept."

His eyes widened and his fingers snapped. "The lady with the boyfriend who wanted to slam his fist into my face!"

Wait, *what?* Rachel realized that the guy had been drinking. He was weaving a bit on his feet. So maybe his drunken state would explain his confusion about Dylan. "He wasn't my boyfriend." She thought it was best to be clear about that. "And I don't think he wanted his fist anyplace near your face."

"He did." The blond nodded as bodies slipped past them. "I can tell. It was in his eyes. The old she's-mine look. I know it when I see it."

Rachel shook her head again. "Maybe you were wearing beer goggles that night." Just like tonight. "He's not my boyfriend," she said again, raising her voice to be heard over the crowd.

"Then maybe I do have a shot." The blond smiled at her. He was a handsome guy, with bright blue eyes and even dimples that flashed. He offered her his hand. "Brent Chastang." He winked. "I'm a lawyer."

An inebriated one. She took his hand, cautiously. She knew what Brent wanted—flirting and a fast hookup. She understood guys like him. But men like Dylan…

I don't want to understand him.

"Does saying that you're a lawyer usually help with the ladies?"

He shrugged. "Sometimes." His shoulders sagged. "Not with you?"

Uh, no. "I was a lawyer, too." She pushed back her hair. "In another life." Then she turned away from him and made her way to the bar. She wanted to sit down and just…soak in the noise and life around her.

She'd thought before that the pub wasn't her scene. But she didn't want to be alone then. Not with pain seeming to squeeze her heart.

Rachel eased up onto the bar stool. Aidan glanced over at her. "Back again, are you?"

Rachel nodded.

He put his hands on his hips. "You scared me the other night."

She winced. "It was just a bump on the head."

"That came when your car was bombed." He edged closer to the bar and to her. "Are you in any kind of trouble? Do you need help?"

"No."

"Tell me the truth," he demanded. "Because if Patrick thought you were in danger and I wasn't helping, he'd roll over in his grave."

His words made her smile. "The only kind of help I need right now… Well, I just need something to make me forget for a little while. I want to relax and be happy." A tall order.

"Tell me the drink, and it's yours."

Hmmm. "I'll have—"

"Look, Ms. I Don't Have a Boyfriend..." Brent's voice was a little too loud as he eased onto the seat beside her. "How about we start all over again?"

Aidan's eyes slid to Brent. "How about I call you a cab?"

Brent blinked. "But I wanted to buy her a drink!" He leaned over the bar toward Aidan. "She's an ex-lawyer, you know. Totally my kind of girl."

Rachel thought all women would fall into the category of being his *kind*.

"Thanks, Brent," she told him, giving him a smile. "But I'm not looking for any sort of hookup tonight. I'm getting a drink, then I'm going home—alone."

"Oh." Disappointment flashed over his face, but he rallied quickly. He pulled out a business card. Put it on the bar in front of her. "If you change your mind, you can always find me here." He winked at her.

Right.

Then he wobbled off his chair, his attention obviously caught by a new, fresh target.

Yes, men like Brent were very easy to understand and to dismiss.

It was men like Dylan who could rip a woman's heart right out of her chest.

Sighing, she glanced back toward Aidan.

He raised a brow. "Want me to trash that card for you?" The Irish rolled lightly in his voice.

"Yes." Definitely.

He grabbed it, ripped it up and tossed it. "Done." His eyes gleamed. "Next order of business...a free drink for my grandpa's favorite girl."

"Thank you."

"How about we just try Paddy's Whiskey again," he said as he began to prepare her drink.

Rachel rested her hands on the bar. Her shoulders rolled as she tried to dispel the tension from her body.

"Why do you look so sad tonight?" Aidan pushed the drink toward her.

Someone shouted his name, but he didn't look away from her.

Her fingers curled around the glass. "I don't like being wrong about people."

He tilted his head as he watched her. "But people lie."

She nodded. "They trick you, and you don't see it coming." She took a sip of the drink. It seemed to warm the cold spots inside of her. "I quit my job today." Her eyes widened when she blurted out the words.

He smiled. "Surprising, isn't it? What folks will say to the bartender." He shook his head. "Oh, the stories that I've heard…"

She took a longer sip.

"Your guy isn't going to come storming in here again?"

Maybe. As soon as Dylan discovered that she'd quit the EOD, he might come looking for her.

"I was worried about you," Aidan said, the faint amusement fading from his gaze. "I'm glad you weren't killed."

"Me, too."

"I know a bomb blast when I see one," Aidan added as his voice lowered. "Not some engine malfunction or gas leak like the news is trying to say."

No, it hadn't been. That was just Mercer trying to do damage control and make sure folks in the city didn't panic.

"If you're in trouble, I can help," Aidan told her. Again, someone called his name. He waved them away. "So I say again… What can I do?"

He'd already done it—given her an ear…and a good drink. "I'm all right," Rachel told him. "But thank you."

Aidan gave her another long, slow look then he answered the calls from the other end of the bar.

Rachel finished her drink. Left a hefty tip, then slid back out through the crowd.

She stayed close to the shadows as she made her way to her apartment. Her steps were slow, and tiredness pulled at her. She knew that Mercer had sent a guard to keep an eye on her place. That would just be standard EOD protocol after the blast. Whether she was an agent or not, Mercer would watch after her.

And Dylan?

Her steps slowed. She turned and rested her back against the brick wall of the pub. A small alley snaked down the left-hand side of the building.

She glanced at the alley then looked back across the street. From that alley, a person would have a perfect vantage point to watch her apartment.

And to stay hidden.

Rachel straightened and peered into the darkness of the alley.

Rachel thought she heard a faint sound. The light scuffle of a shoe? "Is someone there?" she called.

No answer but…the scuffle sounded again. A rasp? She tiptoed closer to the mouth of the alley. "Hello?"

Maybe it was an animal. The faint noise could just be a cat getting into some garbage. That explanation made sense.

"H-help…"

The cry was faint, so very faint, but Rachel heard it. She tensed. *"Who's there?"* And where was the EOD guard? She swung around, glancing back at the street behind her.

She didn't see anyone.

"H-help…" A gasp, but she'd definitely heard the words.

Rachel wished that she had her gun with her. Any kind of weapon. But she didn't.

And she also didn't have the luxury of hesitating.

Rachel rushed toward that faint cry.

DYLAN JUMPED OUT of the SUV. He'd grabbed the first vehicle that he found at the EOD, and he'd shot straight to Rachel's place. He'd thought about calling her, but he'd been afraid the woman would just hang up on him.

She was furious, he got that. But he couldn't let her shut him out like this.

He rushed up the steps to her apartment and nearly slammed into Hunter Paxton. Hunter was a new EOD agent, but he was fast catching attention because when it came to the missions, he was single-minded.

"Something I can do for you?" Hunter asked him.

The guy was actually blocking Dylan's path to the door.

"Yeah, get out of the way," Dylan snapped.

Hunter didn't move. "Mercer just called me. Said that you weren't Rachel's commander any longer. It seems she's left the agency."

No. That wasn't happening. "Mercer is misinformed."

Hunter smiled. "I'd hoped so. I like Rachel."

Every-damn-body did. The woman pulled them all in. *She sure pulled me in.*

Hunter slid to the side. "I got on shift about twenty minutes ago. I was told to watch the building. To make sure access to the place is limited." But then Hunter shook his head. "Save yourself the trouble of racing up there. Rachel hasn't come home yet."

What? If she wasn't home, then where the hell was she?

SHE SAW THE legs first, sprawled out near the garbage container. Legs and—

Rachel gasped as her penlight fell on the figure there. "Brent?"

His shirt was wet with blood. He was gasping and struggling to speak.

She'd just left him minutes before! How could this happen? *How?*

She yanked out her phone. "I'll get help." She'd have an ambulance there in no—

He grabbed at her hand. *"Help..."*

"I am! I'm getting you help." The line rang. Once. Twi—

Brent gasped again. *"G-go..."* He jerked on her. Harder.

And something sharp stabbed into Rachel's neck. The phone fell from her fingers as she spun around, but the man there was cloaked in shadows.

She tried to lunge to her feet, but Rachel felt her body collapsing.

He drugged me.

That sharp prick had been a needle. And...and she'd been drugged before. Three years ago. By Jack.

A needle to her neck. They'd been dancing. She'd trusted him so completely. He'd lifted his hand and injected her. She hadn't seen the needle until it was too late.

Just like it's too late now.

His arms wrapped around her when she collapsed. The drug seemed to instantly weigh down her limbs.

"Don't worry about him, sweetheart. He's already dead." He lifted her easily into his arms. Rachel's eyes were sagging closed but she saw that he had on a dark ski mask. His features were covered. There were holes for his eyes. His gloved hands tightened around her. "And you...you're mine."

DYLAN BURST INTO the pub. Rachel had gone there a few nights before, so maybe she'd tried the place again. He scanned the booths, rushed into the back rooms, and even checked the ladies' bathroom. A few shouts and curses greeted him, but there was no sign of Rachel.

He headed back to the pub's entrance. His body was tight with worry. He tried calling Rachel, but her phone just rang and rang.

Okay, she could be furious at him, but she didn't get to go off the grid like this.

Jaw locking, he turned from the crowd and phoned the EOD. When his call was answered, he snapped. "This is Dylan Foxx." He knew the voice-recognition software would be confirming his identity. "I want a track put on Agent Rachel Mancini's phone. I need the phone's location now." Rachel also had a tracking chip implanted *on* her, but he didn't push for intel on that, not yet. Mercer would need to approve that sort of information retrieval.

Calm down. The order whispered through his mind. He knew it was possible that he was way overreacting.

She's just letting off steam. You know Jack won't hurt her. He saved her life before the blast.

But Dylan couldn't seem to get calm. Fear snaked through him, and Dylan wasn't used to fear.

He only felt fear when Rachel was in danger.

All of his primal instincts were fired up right then.

The agent was back on the line in moments. Dylan put his hand up to his ear, trying to dim the noise so he could hear what Helen Grant had to say. "Triangulation shows that you should be right near Rachel Mancini," Helen told him.

He spun around, searching the bar once more. "Check that signal again and call me back." He shoved the phone into his pocket. He'd just caught sight of the bartender. The guy was laughing as he headed toward a back room.

Dylan pushed people out of his way and grabbed the guy's shoulder. "Aidan, right?"

The guy frowned at him. Then his brows lifted. "Ah, I figured you'd be in, sooner or later." He looked over Dylan's shoulder. "But I think you just missed her..."

"Rachel." Her name burst from him. "She was here?"

Aidan nodded. "Sure. About ten, maybe fifteen minutes ago." Then he added, "She was upset."

Dylan's guts twisted. "I need to find her."

"Yeah, well, good luck with that. I'd suggest you hurry. A pretty lady like her, the guys were already circling in. Especially that jerk, Brent."

"Brent?" He had no idea who Brent was.

Aidan glanced toward the back room then he looked at Dylan once more. "Yeah, the blond who was hitting on her the other night. The guy can't seem to take no for an answer."

"Where. Is. He." Dylan's words were a lethal demand.

Aidan scratched his chin and looked around the pub. "I cut him off, so I think he must've stumbled out…"

But Rachel's phone was still transmitting a signal. One from very, very close by.

He spun away from Aidan.

"Is everything all right?" Aidan called.

Dylan rushed back outside. Her building waited to the left. If she'd left fifteen minutes ago, she would've been home. He started walking, heading on the same path she should have taken.

He stopped in front of the alley. Its interior was dark, cavernous.

"Rachel?" He shouted her name.

There was no answer to his cry.

He looked back toward her apartment.

She hadn't made it that far.

Dylan advanced into the alley, his body tense with adrenaline. He eyes adjusted to the darkness. He could've pulled out his phone and used it as a light, but he didn't want to give away his location. Not until he realized what he was facing.

He'd always had good night vision—far better, in fact, than average. So it was easy enough to make out the bulk of the garbage container.

And to see the body lying beside it.

He ran toward the body and his foot stamped down on something hard. Something—

He bent. *A phone*. Her phone?

Triangulation shows that you should be right near Rachel Mancini.

He bent over the body, and touched the man's throat. No pulse.

Dylan straightened and whirled in the alley. He shouted for her. *"Rachel!"*

WHEN HER EYES OPENED, Rachel found herself in a dark room. She was slumped in a chair. Her hands bound behind her. Her legs were tied, one to each wooden chair leg.

"I learned…from last time." His voice drifted to her. "It's better to make sure that you're securely restrained so I had to tie your legs this time, too."

She'd known he was there. "Same routine, though, right?" Rachel managed. "Drug me. Kidnap me." Her voice sounded a little sluggish. Probably from whatever drugs he'd given her. The drugs would also explain why her mouth was so dry.

But she would *not* let him see or hear her fear. That was what he wanted. To control her. To terrorize her.

"Hey, at least you didn't wake up in the back of my trunk like you did last time." Footsteps shuffled toward her.

She squinted her eyes, but she couldn't see him clearly. It was too dark. Was he still wearing the ski mask?

"I missed you," he told her.

She shook her head.

"And I think, if you look down deep enough, you'll realize that you missed me, too."

She didn't need to look anywhere. "You're insane."

He laughed. "See, *that's* what I missed. Other women would—and have, by the way—begged me at this point. They'd offer anything if I'd just let them go. But not you. You're not like that. You never beg for anything, do you, sweetheart?"

She yanked at the ropes.

"You tricked me." Now a hint of anger hummed through his words. "I was always so careful, watching you. Making sure that you didn't think about turning to another. Then you and…Dylan Foxx. You went out and you put on the show and you made me think that you were involved."

Her heart slammed into her chest. She didn't even want him saying Dylan's name.

"But you have no other lover, do you, Rachel? That was all for show. And now you've left him behind. You've left the EOD, and you've come back to me."

How did he know what she'd done?

She strained again and felt the warmth of her blood as the ropes cut into her wrists.

"I don't like that you tried to deceive me."

Now it was her turn to laugh. "Really? When you're the one who taught me how to lie?"

Silence, then he murmured, "I guess I did."

She kept her breathing low and even. "If you're going to kill me, just do it."

He touched her then, sliding the back of his hand over her cheek. "Killing you isn't on the agenda."

Her racing heartbeat slowed down.

His hand pulled away.

"But I will have to punish you."

And, in the darkness, she saw the gleam of a knife too late.

THE ALLEY WASN'T dark any longer. It seemed to be lit with a thousand lights.

Brent Chastang was dead. According to the M.E., the

guy had bled out quickly from his stab wound, probably only surviving a few moments.

The phone *was* Rachel's. She'd been at the scene.

The bloody playing card that they'd found shoved in Brent's shirt told them that Jack had been there, too.

"Agent Foxx, are you all right?"

He turned at the soft question and found Noelle Evers walking toward him. The EOD had a crime-scene team checking over every inch of the alley. The local cops were being held back until they could finish processing the scene.

"No," he told her, voice clipped. "I'm damned well not." Fury spiked then. He caught her arm and pulled Noelle away from the others. "You said she was safe, that he wouldn't hurt her." He'd been so certain that Noelle was right.

Noelle shook her head. "I never said that."

His teeth snapped together. The fury raged hotter inside of him.

"Hurting her is a definite possibility."

The woman was shredding him.

"But he *won't* kill her. I don't think that he can."

He had to swallow twice before he could talk. "So he's just going to torture her for hours. Then what? Let her go?"

Noelle shook her head. "You already know that won't happen."

"What will he do?" She was the one who was supposed to know. She had to tell him.

"He took Rachel because he wants her with him. I don't think he ever intends to let her go."

No. No. *No!* "It was supposed to be me." That had been the whole point. The reason he'd moved heaven and earth to get her off the case. Rachel should've been safe. Jack was supposed to come after *him*.

"I don't think Jack is done with you. Not yet. He's just made sure that you can't be with Rachel."

But he *needed* to be with her. Dylan clenched his hands into fists because his fingers were trembling. He couldn't afford to show any weakness, not then. He didn't know who might be close.

There'd been no sign of a struggle in the alley. Rachel had simply appeared to vanish.

But I know that didn't happen.

His phone began to ring then. He yanked it from his pocket, wondering if the EOD had news—

Blocked Number.

He stilled.

"What is it?" Noelle asked him softly.

"Personal call. Excuse me." He turned from her and took a few more steps away from the scene. Dylan didn't know why he was hiding the truth from her. He only knew—

I need Rachel back.

"Dylan Foxx." He answered the call when he was sure no one else could overhear him.

"You're not very good at following orders…"

That chilling rasp filled Dylan's ears.

"I think I told you to come *alone* last time, but you just had to drag my Rachel with you."

She's not yours.

"She's bleeding now. She's hurting. And it's all your fault, Agent Foxx."

No. The thunder of Dylan's heartbeat filled his ears. "I'm going to kill you."

Laughter. Low. Insidious. "Is that the way a government agent should talk? Shouldn't you be interested in bringing me in? *Containing* me?"

"Put Rachel on the line." His grip was about to shatter his phone.

"No. I'm afraid that just can't happen."

"Then you don't have her." *Or she's dead.* No. He *wouldn't* go there. "Unless I hear her voice, we're done talking—"

"I have her. You *can't* track her. Oh, I bet you tried, didn't you? Using those EOD connections of yours. But Rachel's' tracking system is…off-line now."

Yes, it was. And that had terrified him.

"She's such a tough marine, isn't she? Rachel didn't even scream when I cut the tracker out of her shoulder."

The image flashed though his head. "Don't *touch* her again."

"I'll touch her plenty. And if I want, I'll use my knife again. I'll see if I can make her scream. I bet if I try hard enough, I can."

Dylan fought to hold back the fury and the fear, but the emotions were choking him.

"Good old Brent was a free kill. I don't usually do those. I like to get paid for my services, but I didn't like the way he kept bothering Rachel."

He'd been in the bar. He'd seen Rachel.

"I figured he deserved what he got." There was a pause. "Just as you deserve what's coming."

"But Rachel doesn't deserve to be hurt." Dylan had to make the guy focus his fury—*on me*.

"I decide what she deserves." His breath sighed out. "I know you were playing a game. You and Rachel aren't together. It was just bait, to lure me in." That low laughter came again. "Good try. But the game's over now. Guess what? I win."

The hell he did. "Ask Rachel. She'll tell you that we're lovers."

He heard a gasp behind him and spun to see Noelle staring at him. Damn it, she'd been eavesdropping.

And he had to wonder just how the profiler had learned to move so soundlessly.

"You're lying!" Anger blasted through Jack's words.

"No, I'm not. It wasn't bait for you. Rachel is mine. She'll tell you."

Noelle began to frantically shake her head.

Dylan's heart iced. His mind worked quickly as he tried to figure out what to say—

"Rachel doesn't give a damn about you," Jack growled.

Maybe she didn't.

"Why did you call?" Dylan demanded. Not just to torment him. But more. There had to be *more*.

"Because I'm not quite done with you."

Dylan's muscles were so tense they ached. "I'll follow orders this time."

"You have to, or else she dies."

He still hadn't heard Rachel's voice. He was straining, desperately trying to pick up some background noise, but there was nothing for him to hear.

"If you tell anyone else, I'll know. I'll see them coming, and I *will* put a bullet in Rachel's head."

"Don't!" The word burst from him too quickly.

Noelle gave another frantic shake of her head.

There was a sharp inhalation on the other end of the line. "Agent Foxx, it sure sounds to me like you care too much for my Rachel."

He did.

"I remember you now," Jack continued. "You *and* Shannon. You don't want Rachel to wind up like Shannon, do you?"

"No," he gritted out from between clenched teeth.

"Then get in your car. Head to the National Harbor. I'll call you again when you're on the way."

"What happens when I get to you?" But Dylan knew just what he planned to do. *Jack, you're a dead man.*

"Isn't it obvious?" Jack murmured. "One of us lives, and one of us dies." A pause. "Now get in the damn car."

The line went dead.

He stared into Noelle's eyes. She knew what was happening. He brushed by her, but Noelle grabbed his arm. "Don't! He'll kill you long before you have any chance of getting to Rachel."

Dylan pulled from her. "My job is to take down Jack. That's exactly what I'm going to do." *And I'm getting Rachel back.*

"He's just going to kill you. You *know* that." Her voice was low, pitched to only reach his ears. "You… you shouldn't have said that you and Rachel were really involved. He was just calling to taunt you, but that changed things for him."

"He's *hurting* her." No one hurt Rachel. No damn one.

"He'll have a trap set for you. Please, Agent Foxx, think about this! He's got this all planned. You know he isn't an average killer."

"That's why the EOD is after him." Because they knew just what sort of threat he posed.

"You need backup!"

"What I need…" He leaned in close because Thomas was coming toward them, and Dylan didn't want the guy catching his next words. "I need her. Safe. Away from him. And I'll do anything in order to get her back."

Then he pulled from her. He stalked away from the alley that smelled of blood and death. He jumped in the SUV that he'd taken from headquarters earlier, and he spun out of the parking lot with a squeal of his tires.

RACHEL COULDN'T SPEAK because of the thick gag in her mouth. All she could do was listen to Jack as he taunted Dylan…and as the killer set the trap to lure him in.

When the call ended, Jack came back to her. She didn't see the knife in his hand. He'd used it on her moments before he'd called Dylan.

"The agent said you were lovers."

Rachel didn't move. He was just a shadow before her. A big, hulking—

A bright light flashed on, illuminating the area. They were in…an office. One that looked as if it was under construction. There were gleaming windows to the left and fresh Sheetrock to the right. Rachel inhaled and caught the scent of—

The river? A faint breeze blew through the window, bringing that scent to her. Jack had said that Dylan needed to drive toward the harbor, and now she realized just how close she was to the water.

She could even hear the lapping of the river outside that window.

"Was he lying? Tell me, Rachel, *was Agent Foxx lying?*"

She nodded and stared up at him. He still had on the ski mask. All she could see were his eyes. Eyes that were burned into her memory.

The knife came up and pressed against the side of her face. She tensed.

But he just cut away the gag. It fell from her mouth, and Rachel licked her parched lips.

"Tell me," Jack demanded. "Say it."

"H-he was lying…"

He stumbled back.

"He was lying," Rachel said again, her voice stronger.

Because she knew exactly what Jack would do if he didn't think Dylan's words were a lie.

"He was lying," she whispered and she prayed that Jack believed her. Because if he didn't…

Dylan and I could both be dead.

NOELLE WATCHED DYLAN rush away. He couldn't do that. He couldn't just go straight into danger.

Into death.

She realized that the EOD wasn't like the FBI. The FBI was all about rules and regulations. Paperwork. Enough files and forms to choke her.

And the EOD…the agents there seemed to be on a constant adrenaline high. They loved the risk and the battles.

Being in the field was the work they craved.

"What's wrong?"

It was *his* voice. Thomas Anthony. He was beside her. Not touching her. He was always so careful not to touch her.

But he seemed to watch her a lot. Noelle knew… because she found herself watching him, too.

"I need to speak with Mercer." She had to tell him what was happening. All of the EOD agents had trackers implanted on them. When she told Mercer what was happening, they could activate Dylan's tracker. Rachel's hadn't worked, but...*Dylan's will.* "Dylan...he just got a call from Jack. He's going after the killer, *without backup.*"

Thomas seemed to absorb that. But instead of immediately sprinting toward a car—and to go follow Dylan—he said, "Who says he needs backup? The man knows how to handle himself."

Shocked, she could only shake her head. "He's walking straight into the killer's trap."

"Dylan is hunting a man that he's wanted to kill for years. It wouldn't be wise to get in his path now."

Noelle backed up a step. "Mercer can activate Dylan's tracker. We can all follow the signal. Go in. Take Jack down."

Thomas shook his head. "The instant that Jack sees anyone else there, what do you think he'll do?"

She hesitated.

"Come on, *profiler.*" The title was almost a taunt. "Tell me, what will he do when he sees more agents?"

Her skin iced. "He'll kill."

"Who will he kill?"

"Dylan." Thanks to the profile she'd created, she could see what would come all too easily. "If he thinks he can't escape, Jack won't go in alive." He had a narcissistic personality, one that thrived on control. On power.

Prison would take that power from him.

In his last moments, Jack would want to assert himself. He'd want the end to be *all* about him. He wouldn't live in a cage.

And he won't let Rachel go again.

"He'll kill Rachel," she whispered. "Then himself."

Thomas nodded "And *that's* exactly why we don't make the call to Mercer right now. We give Dylan time."

But time to what? To kill?

Or to die?

Chapter Eight

The new building complex waited right on the water-front. The scent of the river teased Dylan's nose as he advanced.

The building was about three stories high. Dylan suspected that Jack would be up on the top floor. A better vantage point. A better spot to watch and see if Dylan followed orders.

This time, he had. With Rachel's life on the line, Dylan wouldn't take any chances.

Jack had called him during the drive over. He'd given him terse instructions so that Dylan would locate this exact building. There were quite a few new buildings going up near the harbor. And, this late at night, all of those spots were empty.

Perfect for Jack.

Dylan had listened. Then he'd followed.

Now he advanced toward the building. The main entrance was locked, so he kicked in the door.

The stairwell was dark. But he made his way up. One flight. Two. Three.

The heavy metal door swung open beneath his hands, and he slipped out onto the third floor. It was dark up there, the only light coming in from the moonlight that spilled through windows.

About ten windows lined the left wall. Half of them had already been framed and had glass set in place. The other five were just gaping rectangles that opened into the night.

A breeze blew against him. He had his gun in his hand, gripped tightly. His steps were soft. Careful.

Bright light flooded on above him.

Dylan froze.

"You did better this time," a hard voice called out.

And then Dylan saw them.

A man stood to the left, positioned in front of a gaping rectangle that would one day be a window. A black ski mask covered his face. His left forearm curved around Rachel's neck. And he had a gun pressed to her temple.

"This is the point when you drop your weapon," Jack said.

Dylan put the weapon on the floor.

Jack laughed. "All of your weapons. I'm sure you have backups, right? A good EOD agent would. Probably a knife in your boot. Maybe another gun strapped to your ankle."

He had both. Dylan bent and pulled out the weapons. He tossed them aside. Then he lifted his hands. "There's nothing else."

Helplessly, his gaze went to Rachel. Her face was pale and her eyes were wide, but she showed no emotion.

"You've been a thorn in my side for years, Agent Foxx."

Dylan kept his hands up. He took a slow step forward. "Maybe you shouldn't have decided to make a living by killing. I would've stayed out of your way then."

Jack shook his head. The gun never moved from Rachel's temple. "You do the same thing that I do. Kill. Hunt. For a price. Only you work for the government." Jack shrugged. "And I'm a free agent."

"We're *nothing* alike."

"Are you so sure? Shannon thought we were…"

Dylan's jaw locked.

"Shannon told me that you were a killer. Cold-blooded. Single-minded. The missions were all you cared about. You existed only for the rush."

Shannon *had* told Dylan something similar during one of their last meetings. That he was too focused, too secretive about his work.

But he'd been a SEAL before he'd become an EOD agent. Secrecy was just a part of his life.

"I lived for that rush, too. It's powerful, isn't it? Knowing that you control someone else's fate so completely."

"I'm not in it for the control."

"No? I don't think I believe that, but I don't suppose it matters. What matters…is that I control your fate now. Yours and Rachel's."

"You don't want to hurt Rachel." Dylan forced himself to keep his voice low, calm. A hard task when he wanted to shout his fury and attack. But if he moved too soon, Rachel could be hurt. Killed. "We both know that."

"Do we?" Jack's words mocked him. "You know who I *did* enjoy hurting?"

"Stop," Rachel whispered. Her hand lifted and jerked against Jack's forearm.

He just tightened his grip on her. "I enjoyed killing Shannon. Whiny, demanding Shannon. She was the one who approached me in the bar that night, did you know that? She hit on me. Made my job so much easier. She wanted to hook up with a stranger, with anyone… anyone but *you*."

"Let Rachel go," Dylan demanded.

"So I took Shannon home with me. We became lovers. I let her live a bit, even though I already had the money for her death. But she was useful, despite that whining. She was the one who first told me about the EOD after all." His head shook. "I guess you revealed a little too much to her during your pillow talk."

"Dylan, you shouldn't have come here!" Rachel suddenly shouted. "He's just—he's messing with you! He's going to kill you!"

He can try. Dylan took another step closer to them. He hadn't turned over all of his weapons, and Dylan was just looking for the perfect moment to strike.

"You know, I can't help but notice…" And Jack backed up a step, getting closer to that gaping rectangle that opened to the night. "You didn't seem so upset over Shannon. Or at least, not as upset as I imagined. Would it change things if I told you that she screamed for you at the end? That she begged me to let her go because she realized that she did love you?"

Dylan had locked down his emotions. He *wouldn't* respond to Jack's taunts. He had to focus on the coming attack. Jack wasn't escaping this night. There was no way that he'd let the man go.

"Maybe it's because you've moved on now, hmm? Is that it?" Jack's forearm tightened even more around Rachel's neck. If he wasn't careful, he'd choke her. *Maybe that is the SOB's plan.*

"You sure seemed focused on my Rachel," Jack continued. Anger threaded through his words. "Even going so far as to say that you were lovers."

"We are." His turn to bait the killer. To push Jack over the edge. When the man lost control, Dylan would attack.

Provided that loss of control doesn't risk Rachel.

His gaze darted to her face once more. She was so beautiful. And…and there were tears in her eyes.

Rachel…crying? No, that wasn't right. Rachel never cried.

"I'm sorry, Dylan," she whispered.

"Yes, Dylan," Jack mocked. "She's sorry because the truth is that Rachel never cared for you. In her heart, there's room for only one man, and that man has always been me. All of this time—me." And he moved the gun from Rachel's head. He eased his hold on her throat.

But Rachel didn't try to attack him. She didn't break free of his slackened grip. She just stood there, her body pressing back against Jack.

Jack bent his head and brushed a kiss to her temple, right over the spot he'd pressed his gun seconds before.

"She didn't kill me when she had the chance. You know that. Rachel knows it. I *know* it. You don't kill the one you love."

Dylan stared at Rachel now, not Jack. What in the hell was happening there?

"Tell him, Rachel. Tell him how you feel."

"I belong with Jack," Rachel said.

Jack aimed his weapon at Dylan. "Did you ever love him, sweetheart?"

"No." A tear slipped down her cheek. "I never loved him. Because he isn't you."

Her words hit him harder than a bullet. Rage cracked through Dylan's careful control.

"Good. Very good." Jack pressed another kiss to her temple. "And now that we've got that cleared up, it's time for you to die, Agent Foxx." His eyes glittered. *"Because you never should have touched what is mine—"*

Dylan lunged forward. He knew Jack was about to pull the trigger on that gun and there wasn't any time for hesitation.

But Rachel spun around. She grabbed Jack, hit him hard, and they both fell right through the gaping rectangle of the window frame. They tumbled out of the building and headed for the water below.

The gun discharged as they hit the dark water. *"Rachel!"* Dylan screamed. He couldn't see her or Jack.

Dylan jumped through that window frame and went into the water after her.

His body plummeted into the cold water. It was pitch black beneath the surface, and the current pushed at him.

He pushed back. His hands swept out, searching desperately to try and find Rachel. He kicked up, sucked in a deep gulp of air, and yelled her name. "Rachel!"

His gaze scanned to the left, to the right. He saw a flash of a hand. Then the hand vanished beneath the water.

Dylan dove. He kicked with all his strength, heading to the right. He wasn't leaving Rachel in the water. He wasn't—

Strong hands grabbed him and a forearm locked around his throat. Jack had a chokehold on him, and the two men sank deeper into the water as they struggled.

This was the point when most would probably panic.

Fight harder, rougher, to get out. But that would just waste oxygen.

And it damn well wasn't Dylan's first time in the water. He'd trained and fought—over and over again—in the depths during his SEAL days.

So he didn't waste time in a desperate battle. Instead, he let his body go limp. He wanted Jack to think he was winning that fight. He wanted the jerk to believe that Dylan was dying.

They sank, heading down deeper. Deeper.

Dylan waited for the instant when Jack would ease his grip, thinking that he'd won. He waited—

Jack's forearm slid away from his throat.

Dylan instantly spun around. He shoved his hands into the man's stomach. Then Dylan punched up with his fist, driving right for the man's face. Bubbles exploded from Jack's mouth as he screamed.

Bad mistake.

Now the guy was choking on water.

Dylan's lungs hadn't even started to burn.

Jack flailed as he tried to rush up to the surface and to air. But Dylan caught him. *He* held Jack tightly, easily subduing him.

And when they broke the surface, Jack was the one who was limp and barely breathing.

Dylan immediately shouted, "Rachel!"

Rachel was a strong swimmer, too. She should've been there, waiting at the surface with him.

She wasn't.

He'd been fighting Jack, while Rachel— *No, no, she's okay. She has to be okay.*

"Dylan!"

His head whipped to the left. He knew that voice—it

was Thomas. Thomas dove into the water and broke the surface almost immediately. Dylan shoved Jack toward him. "Keep this SOB contained."

He whirled back around. *"Rachel!"* This time, her name was a roar. Pain twisted through him. He was sure that he'd seen her hand a few moments before. About five yards to the right. Just before Jack had grabbed him.

Dylan dove. It was so dark, he couldn't see anything. His hands swept out. Searching. Desperate.

How long had she been under?

The gun had discharged just when they'd hit the water. Had the bullet hit Rachel?

No, no, no.

Fear wrapped around him and held tight. He wasn't going to leave that water without her. Either he'd find her or—

I won't leave.

His fingers swept out. He touched something then, something soft, silken.

Hair?

Rachel.

He shoved forward and caught her. He pulled Rachel against him and kicked for the surface.

It was okay now. Everything was fine. He'd gotten Rachel. They were both *fine.*

When they broke the surface, he sucked in a gulp of air.

Rachel…didn't.

"No!" He screamed and twisted her in his arms. Her eyes were closed. Her lips closed. "Rachel!"

He swam for the dock, holding her tightly. Fear swallowed him. *Consumed* him. This couldn't be happening. Not to her. Hell, *no.*

He reached the ladder attached to the dock. He pulled her up, and she was limp in his arms.

"What have you done?" The shout came from Jack. He was on the dock, held tightly by a soaked Thomas.

Dylan carefully put Rachel down. "Baby, please, come back." Because she was gone. He could feel it. His heart was like ice.

There was a gasp, then Noelle Evers rushed to his side. "How long was she under?" Noelle whispered.

He swept Rachel's mouth. There was still some water inside, so he turned her onto her side then, when she was clear, he tipped back her jaw. No breath stirred from her, so he put his mouth on hers.

He'd give her his breath. He'd give her everything.

She just had to come back to him.

I never loved him.

He knew, he damn well knew, when Rachel lied. Because he knew her, inside and out.

He checked for a pulse. Found nothing.

He heard Noelle calling for help.

Jack was shouting Rachel's name again and again.

Dylan started chest compressions. She felt so small beneath his hands. Sometimes he forgot how delicate she was because Rachel was always such a powerhouse of energy.

She wasn't breathing.

He breathed for her again. He'd keep breathing for her as long as it took because he wasn't going to let her go. Rachel couldn't do this to him.

He pressed against her chest once more.

She choked. Her body spasmed and water poured from her lips.

Dylan grabbed her and turned her onto her side once

more, holding her as tightly as he could. She was back. *Back.* And he'd never let her go again.

Trembles shook her slender frame. When the water stopped spilling from her lips, he pulled her back against him, wrapping his arms around her and curving his whole body over hers.

He kissed her head. "Don't ever leave me," he whispered. His hold was too tight on her, he knew that, but Dylan couldn't ease his grip.

He'd just fought death for her. He knew that he would fight anything and everything for Rachel.

She didn't speak, but her fingers threaded through his.

There was silence on that dock. Jack had stopped screaming.

Dylan glanced up.

Thomas shoved the killer down to his knees. "Damn, Rachel, you just scared the hell out of me," Thomas said. Since very little ever seemed to scare Thomas, Dylan knew that was a big admission.

And he also knew that he felt the same way.

Then Jack started to laugh. The sound was chilling.

"It's not over…" Jack told them. "It's just starting…"

Dylan rose, keeping Rachel in his arms. The guy had lost his ski mask. His head was bowed, so Dylan couldn't see his face clearly. "You're going to spend the rest of your life in a cage."

Jack tilted his head back. "Don't be so sure of that."

Dylan found himself staring down at a familiar face. The face he'd seen in O'Sullivan's pub. The face of the man who'd seemed so concerned about Rachel hours before.

The man who'd kidnapped her.

Aidan O'Sullivan.

RACHEL SAT IN the back of an ambulance with a blanket around her shoulders. The EMTs had checked her out about five times now, and her body had finally stopped shaking.

"Are you all right?" The soft question came from Noelle. Noelle had been by Rachel's side during all of those EMT checks. The woman was still watching her like a hawk.

Rachel nodded. "Jack's in custody. He won't hurt anyone else again." She swallowed. Her throat ached. Probably due to all of the water that she'd swallowed. "So, yes, I'm definitely all right now."

She wouldn't think about the dark water or about the burn in her lungs. She'd gotten tangled in some kind of rope down there. She'd managed to break the surface once, to wave for help, but the rope hadn't let her stretch out enough to actually suck in air.

So she'd gone back down. She'd fought, twisting and turning, and she'd finally managed to yank her way free of the rope.

There were so many boats docked at the harbor. The rope could've come from anywhere...

And it almost killed me.

By the time she'd gotten free... "I just didn't have the strength to get back to the surface." She'd tried. She'd kicked.

Her lungs had burned.

Rachel exhaled slowly. The last thing she remembered was trying to surge for the surface and then— "Dylan."

Noelle glanced toward a black van that had just arrived on scene. Thomas and Dylan were loading a handcuffed Jack—*Aidan?*—into the van.

I talked to him. I had drinks with him. I never suspected the truth.

Jack had fooled her again.

"When I got here," Noelle said, "Dylan was under the water. You were both down there for a very, very long time."

Rachel's eyes were on the van. On the men there. Jack looked back at her.

He was right in front of me at the pub. And she hadn't recognized him.

Jack had darkened his hair. His nose—it had changed, been broken a time or two. His jaw was different, harder. He must've had some surgery done to alter its appearance. He'd worn contacts, lost weight and changed his voice as he adopted an Irish accent.

He seemed like a totally different man.

But he's the same.

Jack smiled at her. Then he climbed into the van. Thomas followed him inside.

Dylan slammed the door shut. He watched the vehicle as it sped away. His shoulders were tense. When the taillights vanished, Dylan turned back to face Rachel. His gaze held hers. Then he stalked toward her.

Rachel pulled the edges of the blanket closer to her.

Noelle stepped in front of Rachel, blocking her view of Dylan. "Are you afraid of him?"

Rachel shrugged. "Jack's a dangerous man, but showing fear won't—"

"Not him. Dylan."

Maybe she was. He had the power to hurt her more than any other person.

"You are." Noelle seemed surprised.

Rachel glanced up, meeting her eyes. "Even the good guys can be scary."

Noelle glanced over her shoulder. Dylan was just steps away from them now. "You should let the EMTs take you to the hospital for a more thorough check."

Rachel stood. Her clothes were still damp and a chill skated over her flesh. "There's no way I'm stepping foot into a hospital again." She was breathing. She was alert. The EMTs had checked her *five times* for goodness' sake.

"But you need someone to watch you." Noelle's worry was obvious.

"I'll watch her," Dylan said. He brushed by Noelle. He didn't reach out to touch Rachel, and she was glad. Part of her feared that she might shatter if he touched her. "Rachel's coming home with me."

Her eyes widened. "Since when?"

"Since I thought you'd died in my arms… Since I realized that I'm not letting you out of my *sight* tonight." He came even closer to her. His clothes were wet, just like hers, but he didn't seem cold at all. His eyes blazed with emotion. "What the *hell* were you thinking? You went out that window with him!"

Yes, she had. She'd known the water was there, so she'd thought her odds of survival were fair. Her chin lifted. "I was thinking that if I didn't move, you were a dead man. There were only four feet between you and Jack. He wouldn't have missed that shot."

"You mean the way you did? Three years before?"

His question seemed to come out of nowhere, and Rachel flinched.

His eyes widened and a look of what could have

been horror flashed over his face. "No, Rachel, wait, I didn't mean—"

"I'm sure Mercer will want you at the EOD." There would be questions—dozens of them. Reports to write, a massive interrogation to conduct. Jack was the killer, but he'd been hired, paid for his crimes. The EOD would want the names of the people who'd been in contact with him over the years. Now that he was in custody, Jack would become a tool for Mercer to use.

Rachel knew how the game was played.

She was just tired of playing it.

"I don't really give a damn what Mercer wants right now," Dylan said and he put his hands on her. She flinched at his touch because fire seemed to leap through her body.

She'd always been too sensitive when it came to Dylan. Too aware of him. She had to start pulling away from him. The job was done. Dylan had his vengeance.

And she…she could finally stop looking over her shoulder. She could have a real life again.

I never even told my family about Jack. I didn't want them to be afraid. So she'd kept all of the fear to herself.

"I'll…um, let you two talk." Noelle nodded briskly and hurried away.

Rachel didn't want to talk with Dylan, though. She wanted to escape. To collapse.

I want to start building my life again.

"You're what matters to me now," Dylan told her.

Rachel found that she couldn't look in his eyes. So her gaze swept the scene. So many people were there. EOD agents. Techs. "I thought you wanted to get rid of me. That was the whole point in transferring me to Atlanta, right?"

"No." His hold tightened. "The point was to get you away from Jack."

"Then I guess that plan didn't work so well, did it? Maybe we should've stuck to *my* plan, you know, when I said that Jack might try to take me again." And he had. "But you wanted to be the bait."

The plan had gone to hell. They were both just lucky to be able to walk away. "But my idea wouldn't have worked, either," she heard herself whisper. "He knew about the GPS chip. He cut it out of me right away." Her shoulder still throbbed.

"Rachel…"

Enough. She *had* to get away from him. Rachel pulled from his arms. She started walking blindly. Thomas was gone, but there would be another agent on the scene who could give her a ride home.

"I thought you were dead."

Her steps faltered. She was so cold and bone tired.

"When I pulled you out of the water, your body was like ice."

"I got tangled in a rope. Maybe some old netting." She didn't really remember for sure. Rachel looked down at her hands. The nails were ripped. Torn. She'd fought so hard to get free.

"I wasn't coming out of the water without you."

The chill she felt got worse. Rachel shook her head in automatic denial. He was just talking in the heat of the moment. The old EOD code…they didn't leave teammates behind. But *of course* Dylan would've surfaced. He wouldn't have died for her.

With her?

Rachel looked back over her shoulder. Dylan stood, just as she'd left him. His eyes glittered at her. "I wasn't letting you go then." He strode toward her and caught her in his arms. "And I'm not letting you go now." He held her so tightly that she could barely draw in a breath. His head pressed into the curve of her neck, and Rachel felt the shudder that racked him.

"Dylan?" This wasn't like him. Even during their most dangerous missions, he'd never—

"I *can't* let you go, Rachel. I need you too much." His head lifted. "Come with me. Just...*come with me*. Because if I don't keep you close tonight, I think I might go crazy."

There were questions to be answered, statements to be given. The EOD had to clean up the chaos that Jack had left behind. Since Dylan was in charge of this mission, that meant the EOD needed him.

"You should go back to headquarters." She needed to crash.

"He's contained." His voice was a growl. "Everything else can wait a few hours. *You can't wait.*"

Then he had his fingers wrapped with hers. He pulled her away from the scene and toward a waiting car. They climbed inside. Rachel didn't speak. At that point, she wasn't sure what to say.

I never loved you.

Hadn't she already said enough to him?

He cranked the car. A remembered tendril of fear slipped through her, but the engine started easily. They left the harbor.

Rachel wasn't sure what would happen next but she did know that her life was changing.

The EOD was done for her.

Jack was off the streets.

And Dylan? Her gaze slid to him. She'd never seen

him quite like this before. A hard, dangerous edge clung to him and his body was tight with intensity. She had the feeling that his powerful self-control could snap at any moment.

When it did, there would be no going back.

Chapter Nine

"You need to get out of those clothes," Dylan said as he shut the door behind Rachel.

He wanted to touch her again, to pull her against him. He couldn't seem to touch her enough.

She's alive. She's safe.

He had her in his home. Soon he planned to have her in his bed.

Rachel glanced at him. Her eyes were so wide. "I don't… I don't have anything to wear here."

"You can wear one of my shirts." He motioned toward the bathroom. "A hot shower will make you feel better."

"I don't know…" Her voice was hesitant. "I feel like I've already had enough water to last me a lifetime." But she headed for the bathroom.

He locked his muscles and didn't follow her.

She's alive. She's alive. Those words were the mantra that he had to keep repeating to himself.

Because every time he closed his eyes, he saw her, limp in his arms.

Don't leave me.

He raked a hand over his face. He had to make some plans—fast and furious plans. Rachel was going to try and slip away. That couldn't happen.

He'd screwed up. Royally. He'd only been trying to keep her safe, but Rachel wouldn't have seen it that way. She would've thought that he was doubting her abilities. Doubting her.

I was an idiot.

He'd been torn in two. Torn between the leader and the lover.

The lover had won the fight. He'd moved heaven and hell to get Rachel taken off the case. And the lover had been the one to suffer when Rachel stared at him with betrayal in her eyes.

How do I fix this?

Dylan didn't know, but he had to try. He had to do anything, everything, to make her look at him with trust in her eyes again.

He could hear the rush of water from the shower. Good. The water would warm her. Dylan hurried into his bedroom, stripping off his shirt as he went. He could use a shower, too. Actually, he could use a shower *with* Rachel, but that wasn't going to happen.

At least it wouldn't be happening any other place but in his fantasies.

She needs time to heal. She was under the water for too long.

He kicked away his boots. Tossed the socks that clung to him. He reached for the snap of his jeans, but then—then he thought he heard Rachel, crying out.

In an instant, he was at the bathroom door. "Rachel?"

She didn't answer him. He lifted his fist and pounded on the door. "Rachel, are you all right?"

He heard a faint sound. A cry?

Dylan turned the knob. It was unlocked—and he was *in* that bathroom in the next instant.

Rachel was under the spray of the shower. Her shoulders hunched. *Crying.*

His heart twisted. No, the damn thing seemed to break in his chest.

She turned toward him then. His beautiful, strong Rachel. The water slid down her body. "I thought he'd kill you," she confessed.

And he would have died to protect her, in an instant.

Dylan ditched his jeans. He climbed into that shower with her. He wrapped his arms around her and let the water pound down on them both. Her tears ripped into him. He *hated* to see her in pain. "We're safe, baby. It's over for Jack."

"I didn't mean what I said."

Steam rose around them.

"You know that, don't you, Dylan?"

I never loved you.

He swallowed and raised his head. He tipped back Rachel's chin so that he could stare into her eyes. "I know." Then, because he couldn't hold back any longer, because her tears had broken his control and there was no going back for him, Dylan put his mouth on hers.

He'd breathed for her before.

Did she have any clue that he *lived* for her now?

Her arms rose and curled around his neck. Her body—wet, silken skin—pressed to his. Her lips opened. The kiss started soft, but they were both too raw for the gentleness to last.

Passion, need, grew.

His tongue thrust into her mouth. He licked her, tasted—demanded *all* from her.

Just as she demanded everything from him.

His hands swept over her body. *Touch her everywhere. Keep her close.*

He wanted her with him, always.

His fingers caressed her breasts. They were so perfect. They fit in his hands like they were made for him. He lifted her up, holding her easily. He took her nipple into his mouth. Sweet. So amazingly sweet.

She moaned and her hands slid over his back.

He kissed her flesh. Small scars that marked her body. That made him ache because he hated that she'd suffered.

On missions.

Because of Jack.

He kissed her scars again and wished that he could take away her pain.

His fingers were around her waist, holding her up against the slick tile wall. Her legs were parted, and he pushed against her. He wanted inside her more than he wanted his next breath.

Make it perfect for her.

He turned, lifting her from the shower and then letting her feet touch down on the bath rug.

"Dylan?"

He loved the way she said his name. Husky. Sensual.

He yanked on the faucet, turning off the water, then grabbed a towel and took his time drying every perfect inch of her.

He didn't bother wiping the water from his own body. "I was supposed to savor you."

Her breath caught.

"And that's exactly what I'm going to do." It was time to show Rachel that he was a man of his word. He lifted her into his arms and carried her to the bed. He spread her out on the covers then just took a minute to look at her.

Rachel's cheeks were flushed. Her eyes shined. Her lips were red and full. She was wonderfully *alive*.

Her nipples were tight, tipped pink. He slid onto the bed. Covered her but made sure not to crush her body. *Savor*. He would do just that. He wanted Rachel to realize how important she was to him.

He started by stroking her, kissing her. He learned every spot that made her tense. Then he made her gasp with pleasure. He learned how to make her tremble and how to make her ask for more.

Her legs parted for him. He explored her, so aroused that he ached, but he held back.

He brought Rachel to her first climax. She arched against his hand. Moaned his name, and he drank the pleasure from her lips.

For her second climax, *he* was in her, sheathed as far as he could go. He'd pulled away from her only long enough to take care of the protection.

His thrusts grew stronger, harder, and Rachel matched him perfectly. Her eyes were on his. He swore that she could see right into his soul.

Her second release hit, and her inner muscles squeezed around him. He withdrew, thrust, held as tightly to her as he could—

And the world exploded for Dylan. Pleasure hit him, surging over him in the most powerful release of his life.

He kissed Rachel. Held her close.

When the pleasure faded, his head lifted. He stared into her eyes.

"When…" Rachel licked her lips. "Do I get to savor you?"

Dylan found himself smiling down at her even as he thought, *The woman is going to break me.*

THOMAS ANTHONY ENTERED the interrogation room with silent footsteps. Walking silently was pretty much second nature to him, and it was a habit that had come in handy since he'd joined the EOD.

The prisoner in that room was cuffed—both with wrist restraints and ankle cuffs. An armed guard stood behind the assassin known as Jack.

But Jack didn't look intimidated. He glanced up at Thomas, a smile on his face. "I was wondering when the party would get started."

Thomas didn't speak, not yet. He crossed the room and pulled out the chair across from Jack.

Jack's smile widened. "This is a waste of time."

"I don't think so." Thomas didn't glance toward the mirror on the right, a two-way mirror that let those in the observation room watch this little scene play out. "We have your fingerprints, your DNA. In just a little while, we'll know who you really are."

"You already know." A shrug. "I'm Jack."

"You're a killer who hides behind cards." Thomas leaned forward. "You're going to spend the rest of your life in a cage. You'll be damn lucky if you ever see daylight again."

Jack laughed. "Don't count on that…not yet, *Dragon*."

Thomas didn't let his surprise show. Only EOD agents called him by that moniker.

Jack lifted a blond brow. "I guess we all hide behind something, don't we?" Then Jack rolled his shoulders. "But I'm done with this little chat." His hands slammed down on the table and his head turned toward the mirror. "You're watching. Mercer, that's your name, isn't it?" Jack whistled. "If you only knew how much I'd been offered to put a bullet in your heart. Your death…it's always the most requested."

Jack knew far, far more about the EOD than they'd realized.

"I have connections that you can't even dream about," Jack said as he stared at his reflection. "Ties to individuals that I know you'd love to—ah, wait, what's your word? *Contain.*"

"Right now, you're contained," Thomas told him.

Jack's gaze cut to him. "Am I?" He seemed surprised.

What kind of game was the guy playing?

"I have intel." Jack focused on the mirror once more. "Intel that you need. But I'm not just going to spill to the first agent who walks into the room." He straightened. "No offense, Dragon."

What?

"I'll talk to my Rachel, or I won't talk to anyone."

Thomas sighed. He rose from his chair and slowly stalked around the table. Then he brought his face right in front of Jack's. "Do I look like I care what you want?"

"You look like a lackey to me. Someone who doesn't have the power to make a call like this." A smirk was on Jack's face. "You think I don't know how valuable I am? Why do you think Mercer didn't give orders for me to be taken out instead of contained? He wants my intel." Jack shrugged. "And if he wants it, then he's going to have to play by *my* rules."

NOELLE EVERS STARED through the two-way mirror. Mercer was beside her. Silent. Watching.

"He's still trying to pull the strings," Noelle said. Jack's behavior was just as she'd expected. The man was a control freak. Every act, every kill—it was about power to him, not about the money.

"He's also still trying to get Rachel Mancini," Mercer murmured. He glanced at Noelle. "But after what went down at the harbor, how is he going to react if he does see her in person?"

Seeing as how Rachel had pushed the man out a third-story window, probably not so well. "The attachment is still there. If you want to make him talk—" she knew that Mercer did "—then Rachel is your best bet."

Noelle didn't doubt that Jack had secrets to tell. Secrets that Mercer wanted to hear.

The door opened. She glanced over and saw Thomas stalk inside. "He's a smug SOB," he said, disgust in his tone.

He came to stand next to her. Noelle automatically tensed. She did that every time Thomas got too close.

Her job was to profile for Mercer—to watch both the agents at the EOD and the "suspects" that were brought in for questioning. Mercer wanted to make sure that he had no more rogues in-house at the EOD. He also wanted her help at getting into the minds of his enemies.

Since she owed Mercer more than she could repay Noelle had traded in her job at the FBI for some time with the EOD.

And with Thomas Anthony.

She looked up and got caught by Thomas's golden eyes. There was just something about him that was so familiar to her, but Noelle could *not* remember when they'd met.

"Is he bluffing?" Thomas demanded. "Or will the guy actually talk if Rachel comes in?"

She hesitated. "It's a game to him. He wants to be the one who wins."

Thomas shook his head. "That's not an answer. Is the guy going to tell us what we need to know or not?"

Mercer's phone rang then. He answered immediately, moving to the side. *"What?"* She heard him say. "Hell, no, that just makes things harder." He ended the call abruptly and glanced back at her.

"We were right," Mercer said as he inclined his head toward the interrogation room. "The guy is ex-military. His real name is Kenneth Cross. According to the match we just found in the system, that guy was part of the U.S. Army 75th Ranger Regiment."

Noelle knew the situation had just gone from bad to much worse. Kenneth wasn't just a killer, but they'd always known that. His ranger status put him in a whole new category.

"His file said he died in battle." Mercer's jaw hardened. "Guess which senior officer signed off on that death? I'll give you a damn hint. Old *Jack* in there killed him recently."

"William Harris," Thomas muttered.

Noelle focused on the cuffed man once more. He still had a faint grin on his face. "A ranger won't break during interrogation." And this guy…he was exhibiting behavior that made her strongly suspect psychopathic tendencies were working in his mind.

But the attachment to Rachel doesn't fit.

During all of her years of study and her work in the field, Noelle had found that psychopaths rarely formed any sort of real attachment to other people. Others simply didn't have meaning to them. Sure, some psychopaths would mimic the behavior of attachment. They'd go through the motions, but it wasn't real.

"Maybe he'll break," Thomas allowed. "Maybe he won't." He straightened his shoulders. "With your permission, sir?"

Mercer hesitated. His eyes narrowed as he studied Kenneth Cross.

"He's not going to break," Noelle stated again. But... this *was* why Mercer wanted her there. To tell him what she thought. "He'll withstand pain. He might even *enjoy* the pain. He'll like having the power, because he knows he has information that you need."

"He killed so many men and women." Mercer exhaled heavily. "Those victims had some powerful ties in D.C. A lot of folks are wanting answers."

And vengeance.

"Bring in Rachel," Noelle said, her voice soft.

Thomas swore. "You really want to just give that guy what he wants?"

No. She wanted to push that guy to the edge. "Bring in Rachel *and* Dylan." Because it was the dynamic between them all that she needed to observe. The more she watched, the better able Noelle would be to see the chinks in Kenneth's armor. "We already know that Rachel is his weakness. If we want him to break, then we have to use her."

Mercer hesitated then he reached for his phone once more.

DYLAN'S PHONE RANG, vibrating softly on the nightstand. Rachel stirred a bit beside him, but her eyes didn't open. Carefully, he eased his arm from beneath her head. He slipped from the bed, grabbed the phone and crept into the hallway.

A glance at the clock showed him that it was 4:00 a.m. And he knew exactly who was calling him. *"Mercer."* His voice was a snarling whisper. "Why couldn't this wait?"

"Is Rachel with you?"

He glanced toward the open bedroom door. He could just make out the edge of the bed. "Yes."

Silence, then… "I'm going to need you to bring her in."

"Your questions can wait until morning. The woman has been through hell. She nearly *died*—"

"This isn't about getting questions for some report, Agent Foxx. Jack has said that he will only talk with Rachel, and I want you to bring her in. That's an order."

For an instant, Dylan was sure that he'd shatter the phone. His fingers actually ached.

"Agent Foxx?"

He had to unclench his teeth. "I don't give a damn what he wants. That guy *isn't* getting near Rachel." Was Mercer crazy?

"He'll be restrained at all times. And of course I'd expect you to be in the interrogation room with them."

"Not *happening.*"

"Agent Foxx, I understand how you—"

"I don't think you do understand, *Director.*" His breath huffed out. "You don't understand what it's like to think that the woman you…you care about—" he stumbled over those words because there were things he *wouldn't* say to Mercer "—is lost to you. When the whole world goes dark because she's gone, and you know that you can't go on without her."

Silence. Heavy. Thick. Then Mercer said, "I know

exactly how that feels, and I'm sorry, very sorry, that you had to experience it."

His quiet words caught Dylan off guard. He'd heard a few whispers about Mercer's past. Now he knew those whispers weren't wrong.

"But this case is bigger than you and Rachel Mancini. Other lives are involved."

"Rachel isn't even EOD anymore."

"Ah, well, I haven't officially accepted her resignation yet, have I?" Mercer cleared his throat. "I need her here. I need you both here."

Dylan leaned forward and stared into the bedroom. Rachel was sleeping so peacefully. "At 0700," he said, voice clipped. "But I stay at her side, every second." He didn't trust Jack. He'd be happy when the guy was locked away in a maximum-security prison. *The sooner, the better.*

"I'll be waiting," Mercer said.

Dylan ended the call and headed back into the bedroom. He slipped into the bed. He pulled Rachel toward him, cradling her against his chest.

His fingers slid over her back, over the old, carving scar that marked her. Jack had sliced her with his knife three years ago. The man had almost killed her hours before.

She whispered Dylan's name in her sleep.

He stiffened. *Rachel.*

Dylan knew it was wrong, but he didn't care about the other lives on the line. Or at least, he didn't care as much.

The life that mattered to him? It was *her* life. And he'd fight to the death in order to keep her safe.

RACHEL TOOK A deep breath and stared through the observation glass. Jack was on the other side of that glass. Handcuffed and with his ankles also secured in restraints. An armed guard stood behind him.

"He's been like that all night," Noelle said. "And the man shows no signs of any fatigue."

"If he was a ranger," Rachel said, turning to glance at her, "he wouldn't, would he?"

She'd been briefed on Kenneth Cross just a few moments before. Mercer didn't want her going into that interrogation room without as much intel as she could possibly get.

Her monster had a real name now. A real history.

Kenneth Cross. Thirty-five. He'd grown up on a ranch in Montana. His mother had died when he was seven, and his father had passed away in an accident on Kenneth's eighteenth birthday.

Kenneth had joined the army after that, risen quickly through the ranks.

He'd been a ranger when he died, under the command of William Harris. He'd supposedly been killed in a bombing while serving in the Middle East.

Only he sure didn't look like a ghost to Rachel.

"He'll try and control you when you enter that room," Noelle warned her. Noelle's eyes were worried. "You should be prepared for him to say anything. He obviously has some sort of plan in mind, or he wouldn't have insisted on you coming in there."

It wouldn't be the first time a prisoner had tried to manipulate the EOD. Just months before, they'd faced a dangerous terrorist, Anton Devast. Devast had thought that he could manipulate the EOD.

He'd been wrong. He'd died.

Noelle's gaze darted to Dylan. "You have to stay in control."

"Dylan won't have a problem with control," Rachel said, her voice coming out sharp.

Noelle bit her lower lip. "I'm not so sure about that."

Rachel took a moment to study Dylan. His face was completely expressionless and his eyes showed no emotion. "I'm sure of him," Rachel said.

She was. If she hadn't been, then Rachel never would've walked back into the EOD.

Tension drew her shoulders tight. Rachel exhaled slowly and said, "So what's the plan? I just go in there? Question him?" She knew how to handle a normal prisoner interrogation, but this wasn't exactly a normal situation.

"I think he'll do the talking." Noelle's focus appeared to be on Jack. "At first, anyway. You need to break through the facade he has. Get to the real man underneath."

"You mean the killer inside."

Noelle nodded. "I'd...I'd ask about his father."

Rachel's brows climbed even as her stomach knotted. She had a feeling about where this might be headed.

"An accidental death on the guy's birthday." Noelle rocked back on her heels. "That could be quite a present to a psychopath."

"Is that what you think he is?" Dylan asked, a bite to his words. "You're going to give him a label so that what he's done makes more sense?"

Noelle's eyelids flickered. "Kenneth Cross is very unusual. I haven't come across another killer like him before."

"Well, then I guess this will be a learning experience

for us all," Rachel said. *Time to do this.* She wasn't going to cower in the room any longer. And—and *Kenneth* was staring straight through the glass, a faint smile tipping up the corners of his lips. As if he knew that she was there.

The door opened behind Noelle. Mercer stepped inside. "Are we ready?"

As ready as Rachel could get. She headed out first, brushing by Mercer. Two other guards were outside Kenneth's interrogation room. She would've thought that was overkill, but she knew how the guy worked.

One of the guards opened the door for her. Rachel took a steadying breath, tried to wipe the emotion from her face, then entered that small room.

He stood, or at least Kenneth stood as much as the restraints would allow him to do so. "Ah, Rachel…I knew you'd come to me."

Dylan shut the door behind them. "We're *both* here."

Kenneth's face tightened. "You, I could have done without." His eyes stayed on Rachel's face. "Do you feel better today? I'm sorry for what I had to do, but you deserved it, you know. You shouldn't have pushed us into the water."

There were two chairs across from Kenneth. Rachel didn't sit, not yet.

Neither did Dylan. Dylan did walk to the side, though, and he propped his back up against the wall as he stared at Kenneth.

"What you had to do?" Rachel let her brows climb. "You mean drugging me, kidnapping me—"

"Oh, no." Kenneth shook his head. "I mean when I had to wrap the rope around your feet to keep you under the water."

Her skin iced.

"We hit the water together, don't you remember?" Kenneth asked her, a faint frown pulling his brows low. "I was angry at you, sweetheart, so angry, so when I felt the rope, I had to use it. I pulled on it, and when it didn't give, I knew it had to be twisted beneath some old pilings or even an anchor."

"And you tied it around me." She could almost see the image—memory?—now.

He shrugged. "I was going to come back for you, but Agent Foxx over there delayed me."

Her gaze jumped to Dylan. His face still held no expression, but his eyes blazed.

"She nearly died," Dylan snapped.

"Actually..." Kenneth eased back into his seat. "I think she did die for a minute there. I mean, that's why you had to do the whole mouth-to-mouth scene, wasn't it?" His head tilted as he regarded Rachel with curiosity. "What was that like? Did you see the big, white light that people talk about?"

She pulled out the chair across from him, sat down and stared back at him. "Your name is Kenneth Cross."

Anger flashed on his face. "I'm *Jack*."

"You grew up in Montana. You lived on a ranch."

He laughed. "Got a hit on my DNA, huh? Or was it my prints?"

"You were an army ranger, under the command of William Harris."

He leaned toward her. "Don't tell anyone." His voice had dropped to a conspiratorial whisper. "But I think he may be dead."

She gazed into his eyes. "We know who you are now."

Voice still low, he said, "You know nothing."

She thought about the files that she'd read. "I know

that the real Aidan O'Sullivan is dead. I'm guessing that his body will be found eventually, and he'll have a playing card on his chest."

His grin flashed. "He might." Then his laughter came. "But wasn't it a grand cover?" The Irish drifted back into his voice then. "I was in Ireland for over a year. Met Aidan there. He wanted me to kill his grandfather, but I don't just take *any* kind of work."

No. "You like to be challenged."

He nodded. "An old man wasn't going to challenge me. He would've been too easy."

"That's why you focus on ex-military, isn't it?" Rachel asked him. "That way, you have more of—"

"A fight?" He shrugged. "I think it evens the playing field."

"But…Brent Chastang wasn't ex-military."

His jaw tightened. "He was a jerk who needed to stay away from you."

The guard stood, still as a statue, behind Kenneth.

Dylan moved toward the guard then. He whispered to him. The guard hesitated, but then made his way out of the room.

"Just us three?" Kenneth asked. He pursed his lips. "And of course, the ones watching in that little room next door."

Rachel decided to gamble. "There's a profiler in there. She told me that you were a psychopath."

Rage ignited—plain to see—in his eyes. "The profiler would be wrong."

"I don't know…all the people you've killed. Your total disregard for human life—"

"I have regard for life. *Your* life."

Now Dylan stood behind Kenneth.

"It's the others that I don't give a damn about," Kenneth continued. He acted as if what he'd just said was perfectly reasonable. Probably because, to him, it was.

"Did you give a damn about your father?" Was Noelle right? Had he—

His grin flashed.

He had.

"He was a fool who spent too much time caring about the dirt beneath his feet. Like the land mattered. He wanted to hold me back, to keep me out there, when I was meant for more."

"So you killed him," Rachel said, voice hollow. *Eighteen.* He'd killed his father then.

"And I realized that I was very, very good at killing." He glanced over his shoulder. "But I guess that's something that Agent Foxx and I have in common, isn't it? Shannon saw it. And you see it, too." His focus shifted back to Rachel. "Don't you?"

She shook her head. "I don't think you're anything alike."

"You shouldn't be so certain."

Control. The word whispered through her mind. Kenneth was trying to control everything that was said in that room.

She had to stop him.

Rachel surged to her feet. "This is a waste of time. You don't have any intel to give me." She spun on her heel and marched for the door. "And I don't have any more time to waste on you."

"Don't you leave me!"

She reached for the door.

"If you leave me, they'll die."

Rachel stilled. "Who will die?" This wasn't supposed

to be about new victims. She was supposed to be getting the names of all the people who'd hired Kenneth over the years.

Rachel turned to stare at him as she tried to decide if the guy was just playing her.

The smile was gone from his face. He stared at her, cheeks red, mouth tight.

"Who will die, Kenneth?" Rachel pressed.

"My name's Jack!" He shot up.

Dylan's hands came down on his shoulders and he pushed the man right back down.

Rachel didn't advance toward Dylan and the killer. She just stood there, waiting. If he wanted to talk, he would.

And he did.

"Aidan O'Sullivan loved explosions. Loved to light up the night. He learned how to wire the bombs when he was a kid, at his da's knee. But the grandfather… Oh, he was the law-abiding type. That was why he left Ireland. Left them all, and came here."

She didn't move.

"I already had some demolitions know-how, but Aidan taught me a few new tricks." He looked back at Dylan. "I used one of those tricks on your car. It was small, though. Nothing at all when compared to what I've got coming."

She couldn't tell if he was lying or not. "You don't have a target. You wouldn't—"

"As much as I do enjoy you, sweetheart, you aren't the only reason that I came back to the U.S. I had work to do. A job that only a man with my…talents could perform."

"You killed Henry Patterson," she said.

A shrug. "A side deal I picked up. Not my main ticket."

Her heart raced, shaking her chest. "You're lying."

"Am I?" His grin held a cruel edge. "Then by all means, waste a few more hours. When the fire hits the sky, you can believe me then."

A bomb. Had he really planted a bomb in the city?

"Where is it?" Rachel asked him.

But he shook his head. "Doesn't work like that. It's more of a show-and-tell deal."

Her gaze strayed to Dylan. There was still no expression on his face.

"I'll show you where it is…or we can wait, and when all the people die, you can be the one to tell their families just how sorry you are." When she didn't speak, he exhaled on a long sigh. "Still don't believe me, huh? Well, I'm sure the EOD agents are at the pub. Tell them to check downstairs. There's a false wall behind my kegs. They'll find some…leftovers down there. Enough to prove exactly what I'm saying." He laughed. "Or maybe they'll be the leftovers…the parts that are left of them after—"

Rachel ran from the room. Mercer met her outside. He was already on his phone. She heard him say, "Get out of the pub, out of the damn building. Get everyone *out!*"

But would they be able to get them all out fast enough? Or had the agents just walked right into the killer's trap?

Chapter Ten

Dylan walked around the narrow table. He and Kenneth Cross were alone.

And Dylan wanted to kill the man.

Kenneth lifted his brows. "Wishing you'd left me in the water, aren't you?"

Hell, *yes.*

"But then...if you had, all of the agents in the pub would be dead." A pause. "If they aren't already. And that's just the first little surprise that I have planned. Surely you didn't think I'd be unprepared for a—a *containment,* did you?"

"I think you're insane. I think you're not going to tell us the names of anyone who hired you. I think you just want to jerk Rachel around."

Kenneth lowered his gaze as he stared at the tabletop. "I want many things from Rachel."

"Yeah? Too bad. You're getting *nothing* from her."

"Because you think she's yours?" Kenneth didn't sound concerned. He should've. "Shannon was supposed to be yours, too, wasn't she?"

"Rachel isn't like Shannon."

"No, and that's the fun part. At her core, I knew that Shannon was weak. I could predict her behavior. But

Rachel? Ah, now I never can tell what she'll do. In a world of few surprises, she is one."

He wanted to drive his fist into the man's face. Would that be enough of a surprise for this nut?

"Going through the window? Perfect." And he sounded like he meant it. "I never saw it coming, not until it was too late."

The door opened. Rachel was back. Mercer was right behind her. "They barely got out," Rachel whispered.

Mercer pushed past her. "Two of my men are on the way to the hospital. You son of a bitch—*are there more bombs?*"

"Now," Kenneth said, nodding, "I think we all might be on the same page." His gaze swept over Mercer. "So you're the man in charge?"

Control. Noelle had told them that the killer wouldn't give it up. She'd been right.

"I have a very large target in this city. One that I *will* take out…my bombs are already set. But I can be persuaded to show you their locations. I'll take Rachel with me. I'll disarm the bombs and, in return, you will let me just walk away."

"Hell, no," Dylan snapped. The EOD had a standing rule—*we don't negotiate with terrorists.*

Kenneth slumped back in his chair. "Then I guess it's just a matter of us waiting and seeing…who will die next?"

"You aren't going with him," Dylan said as he pulled Rachel into his office and slammed the door shut. "I don't care what Mercer decides—*you can't.*"

Rachel stared up at him. "You're not my team leader anymore."

"You're not even EOD anymore!" he shouted. Then Dylan took a deep breath. He paced the confines of the office, looking very much like a caged tiger. "It's a trap. We all know it. He'll take you to some secluded place, and he'll kill you. If he's got bombs out there, the guy isn't going to disarm them. Hell, he probably just wants to go and watch them blow."

The way the pub had blown? She'd been told there was nothing left of the building but rubble now. "He didn't kill any civilians in the explosion today. He— he could have set the bomb to go off last night, but he waited…"

Dylan stopped his pacing. "You think if we hadn't brought him in, then the guy would have gone back and disarmed the bomb there?"

She nodded and the guilt was *on* her. "I should have come and talked to him sooner. Then no one would be hurt and—"

Dylan lunged toward her and grabbed her arms. "He's insane. He wanted to cover his tracks. That's what he was doing. He set the bomb to blow at O'Sullivan's because he thought he'd be taking you away with him today. He probably planned to kill me then take you away in one of the boats at the harbor. He set the bomb at the pub so all the evidence that he'd left behind would be destroyed. *That's not on you.*"

"But it will be on me if his next bomb kills someone." Her words were soft. Sad.

His grip tightened on her. "Rachel…"

"He's not lying, Dylan. There is another bomb." She'd never been more certain of anything. "He's in D.C. because he has a big target, and he's going to take out that target." He'd moved to take her last night… *Why?*

The answer came to her immediately. *Because he'd planned to take out his real target today. And Dylan was right—Kenneth planned to take me with him when he left D.C.*

"We have to act fast," she said, voice wooden. She knew the risk she was taking. Kenneth could lead her straight to the bomb site and the place could explode around them.

"A bomb squad can go with him," Dylan argued. "We've got plenty of demolitions experts right here in the EOD."

"You know Kenneth won't take them there. He'll only cooperate if I go…or he'll just sit in that little room, and he'll wait for the explosion to come."

The mask fell from Dylan's face. And the first thing that she saw? *Fear.* "I don't want to lose you, Rachel."

She tried to smile for him even though the same fear chilled her veins. "And here I thought you were trying to ship me off to Atlanta."

He flinched. "I'm so sorry…so damn sorry." His mouth crashed down on hers. He kissed her with a wild desperation, holding her tightly. "I wanted you safe. That's all I wanted…"

She kissed him back. Held him just as tightly. She wanted him safe, too, and that was why she'd take any risk. Even falling three floors and nearly drowning. *To protect him.*

His mouth lifted from hers, the barest of spaces. "I want to leave with you. Walk out the door and just *be* with you."

Tears stung her eyes. "That's not who you are." She pushed against his chest. He stepped back.

"No," Dylan agreed. "It's not."

"I'm going to do this." She stared into his eyes. "And you're not going to stop me."

"Rachel, I—"

"Because you know who I am. You know me better than anyone else alive." Her family saw the image that she presented to them. When she visited them in New York, they embraced her in their wonderful, loving arms, but they didn't *know* her. He did. "You won't make the mistake of trying to push me aside this time." He *couldn't.*

His hands had fisted. "What will I do...*damn it, what if you die?*"

"I won't." Her fingers wrapped around his fist. "Because you'll have my back, just like you always do."

His Adam's apple moved as he swallowed. "I know you well," he rasped.

He wouldn't stand in her way.

Rachel turned from him. There wasn't any time to waste. She had to tell Mercer—

"I love you."

She felt the impact of those words roll through her whole body.

"I screwed up before," Dylan said. "I hurt you... because I was so scared. I'm not used to fear. I'm not used to love, either. But...*I love you.*"

Rachel glanced back over her shoulder. "I know."

His eyes widened.

"I know you pretty well, too," Rachel told him softly. "And when I come back—because I am coming back— I'll show you just how I feel about you."

Rachel pulled open the door and hurried into the hallway.

I love you.

His words gave her strength.

Mercer waited for her in front of the interrogation room door. When she approached him, he straightened and said, "You don't have to do this."

She heard footsteps behind her. "Yes, I do." It was time to end this chapter of her life. She wanted the future that waited for her.

She wanted Dylan.

But first, she had to stop the killer in that interrogation room.

Mercer opened the door for her.

Kenneth glanced up.

"Show me," she told him. Because that was all that she had to say.

DYLAN WATCHED AS Rachel drove away. She and Thomas Anthony were in the front of the vehicle. Kenneth was secured in the back. Dylan followed behind them in a separate vehicle, as did several other agents. Demolitions experts.

They were ready for whatever trick Kenneth tried to throw their way.

Because there would be a twist, Dylan was certain of it.

The miles slid past. Soon enough, Dylan realized that they were heading back to the harbor.

"The location makes sense," Noelle murmured from beside him. "He had plenty of access to this place. We know he did."

Dylan yanked out his phone and called Mercer. "Harbor bound," he snapped.

"I'm watching the GPS," Mercer replied. "Already got a crew checking on all the boats there."

Because it would be easy enough for Kenneth to rig a bomb to a boat. The thing could explode when the ignition turned, the same way it had with Dylan's car.

Or the bomb could be on a timer.

"There's a celebration set for the harbor tonight," Mercer said. Dylan heard the murmur of voices then Mercer swore and told him, "Senator Lawrence Duncan has a boat out there. The Dreamer. Duncan's ex-navy. *He* could be the target."

Maybe. Maybe not.

"Stay close, Agent Foxx. Don't lower your guard for an instant."

MERCER PUT DOWN his phone. The whole setup felt wrong to him.

Kenneth Cross is a crazy SOB. He could be planning to light up that whole harbor and kill everyone in his path.

Except…Kenneth liked a challenge.

I have a very large target in this city. One that I will take out…my bombs are already set. Kenneth's words echoed in Mercer's mind.

There were so many potential targets in the city. Powerful men and women who fit Kenneth's attack profile.

Ex-military.

Positioned with connections to all the big players in D.C.

There were senators, generals…

Hell, even the president.

And…

Mercer stared down at his phone.

There's also me.

RACHEL GLANCED BACK at Kenneth. His face appeared calm. He'd spoken only to give them directions. His voice had been quiet, almost mild.

Soon, very soon, they were stopping at the harbor.

Rachel quickly exited the vehicle. Thomas pulled Kenneth from the backseat and kept a tight hold on the man. Dylan and Noelle marched toward them. The other agents hung back.

Kenneth was manacled—hands and feet—and he could only take slow, mincing steps. He should have seemed powerless. He didn't.

"I'm not going to be able to get on a boat this way," Kenneth said, yanking at his cuffs.

"That's because you're not getting on a boat," Rachel snapped at him. She wanted to be done with Kenneth. "We're here, and our bomb-sniffing dogs can do the rest. Your job is *over.*"

Rachel motioned to the van that had just pulled in the lot behind them. The doors opened, and the handlers brought out their dogs.

Dylan's gaze scanned the boats. "Start with the Dreamer," he ordered.

Rachel's brows rose. Why had he picked that boat?

"It belongs to Senator Duncan," Dylan said, glancing her way. "Mercer thinks the guy could be Kenneth's target."

Kenneth frowned at him. "Trying to steal my show? That's not good form, Agent Foxx."

Dylan advanced on the guy. "It's not a show. It's life. We did our part. We let you drag us out here, and now you—"

"Senator Duncan isn't my target, though he is someone that I wouldn't have minded killing." Kenneth tilted his head to stare at Dylan. "But I had a very, very big fish to fry this time. The biggest of my career."

"No…" Rachel whispered as a new fear snaked through her. She stared at Kenneth, hoping, praying that she was wrong.

A very, very big fish.

She grabbed for her phone, dialed the EOD.

"Too late," Kenneth said as he glanced toward her. "I had to get you out of there, of course, before the explosion could commence. Didn't want you getting caught in the blast. It was actually quite tricky to arrange everything, you know…"

I had to get you out of there.

"Mercer!" Rachel's voice shook when he answered the phone. "Get out of the building! Get everyone *out!*" Her words were eerily reminiscent of his own from just hours before.

Kenneth shrugged. "You all gave me the idea with that little tracker under your skin… I learned about that a few months back, and thought, why not use it myself? Those trackers were so clever."

"What the hell is happening?" Mercer demanded in Rachel's ear.

"I think you're the target. Hit the alarm there. Get everyone *out!*"

Kenneth kept talking. "I just had to attract the EOD's attention, had to get your fine, upstanding agents to bring me to your office. And when I knew that Mercer was there, *at* the facility, I just had to signal my employer." He winked at Rachel. "Want to guess what the signal was?"

Dylan lunged forward. His hands clenched around Kenneth's shoulders. "You bastard!"

Kenneth laughed again. "It was a convoy of cars leaving the facility."

There was silence on the line. Too much silence.

"Mercer!" Rachel screamed.

Then the deafening boom burst across the phone line.

The phone slipped from her fingers and hit the ground. She stared at Kenneth, horrified.

But he just kept laughing. "And the Jack just took out the King. The untouchable Bruce Mercer is now little more than a pile of ash."

No, no, he was wrong. He *had* to be wrong.

Rachel bent and scooped up her phone. She called Mercer back. The phone rang and rang.

Thomas signaled to some of the other agents. They jumped in their vehicles, sped away. The demolitions team was needed at the EOD, so they were burning rubber to get back to base.

If anything was left of it.

Dylan dropped his hold on Kenneth, stepped back and heaved in a breath. Then he drew back his fist and punched Kenneth. Kenneth stumbled back and fell—

Just as a bullet flew through the air. It slammed into the dock, sending wood splintering.

Kenneth didn't get up. Blood trickled down his chin. "You're dead, Agent Foxx. You think I would've come back here without backup? I was two steps ahead all along! *Two damn steps!*"

And they were out in the open with no cover.

There were civilians just a few yards away. They'd screamed at the blast of gunfire.

Another bullet blasted out. It hit Dylan, seeming to fly right into his chest.

"No!" Rachel cried.

Dylan fell back into the water.

Thomas grabbed Noelle, shielding her with his body.

The other agents still on scene rushed to protect the civilians.

And Kenneth—he dropped the cuffs. They just fell from his wrists. "Those really weren't as secure as you thought."

More gunfire erupted, thundering all around Rachel, but not hitting her. She froze. The shooter had to be up high and to the right. She turned her head and glimpsed the glint off the weapon.

"He's in our room," Kenneth said as he took care of the restraints at his ankles. "You know that cozy little place I kept you in last night? And this is going to be the really fun part... Guess who it is. Come on, guess."

Another bullet blasted, hitting the wood less than an inch from her right foot.

"Chris Harris," Kenneth whispered. "You should have followed his case a bit longer. You got distracted and, yesterday morning, he escaped from confinement. With a little help, that is." His smile widened. "He owed me big. Not only did I kill the judge, but I took out the bastard father that he hated, too."

Chris's words rolled through her mind. *One way or another, I'm getting out of here! I won't stand trial again—I'm getting out.*

They hadn't realized the guy meant he had an escape plan in place.

She didn't see Dylan. He hadn't surfaced. He *had* to surface.

Kenneth caught her hand. "This is how it ends. You come with me and we get on the Dreamer..." His smile flashed. "I always planned for us to leave on that one.

Senator Duncan…let's just say he owed me, too. For past services. The boat will make us even."

The phone was still in her hand. Still on, so that if anyone was listening on the other end…they'd hear his words.

"Now you come with me, right now, or I'll give the signal for Harris up there to shoot you in the heart."

"The way he shot Dylan?"

"*Dylan was a dead man walking!* But why do you care? You never loved him, you said—"

"I lied," she told him, voice shaking. Thomas was gone. He'd run toward the building. For the shooter? "I lied, and you didn't know me well enough to tell."

Kenneth shook his head. "You didn't kill me. You had the chance. You didn't—"

Rachel dropped her phone once more. When his gaze automatically followed the phone's descent, she yanked out her weapon and pointed it right at his chest. "I won't miss this time."

"*Rachel.*" Kenneth lifted his right hand. "You surprise me. You always have. You weren't what I expected."

She tightened her grip on the weapon. She had to get in the water, had to find Dylan.

Kenneth backed up a step. His left hand also rose, as if he were surrendering to her. "I like that you could surprise me."

No more bullets were being fired. Was that because Thomas had gotten to the shooter? Or because the "surrender" gesture that Kenneth was making actually was just a signal for the shooter to pause?

And what if Kenneth gives him the signal to shoot?

Kenneth took another slow, gliding step back. He was

nearly at the edge of the dock. "I wanted you to be the queen. My Queen of Hearts."

His left hand started to drop.

"Don't!" Rachel screamed.

"But I'm not going into a cage, and if you have to die—" His hands flew down. "So be it. So damn be it—"

Hard arms wrapped around Kenneth's legs, catching him beneath the knees. And Rachel saw Dylan's face appear just above the dock. His expression was locked in lines of fury. Dylan yanked Kenneth back. They both hit the water.

No bullets rained down on Rachel. She spun around, looking up at the window.

"Clear!" Thomas's voice shouted.

Her breath heaved out and she rushed to the edge of the dock. The men broke the top of the water. Fighting, punching viciously.

Then they went back under.

Rachel aimed her gun, ready to take the shot when Kenneth came back up.

But he didn't come back up.

Dylan did. Dylan broke through the surface. He stroked toward her, heaved up on the dock. She helped him, grabbing him tightly. Her arms wrapped around him and she held him close, shuddering because she'd thought he was dead.

This is the way he felt about me.

"I love you," Rachel whispered. "Please, don't ever leave me."

But his body started to sag against her. "Dylan?" Rachel whispered.

He fell back. She staggered beneath his weight and slid down with him.

The sunlight fell on him, showing that it wasn't just water that soaked him. It was blood. "No." She put her hands on him and tried to apply pressure to the wound. "Noelle, *help me!*"

The profiler ran toward her. Rachel heard the other woman, talking on her phone, demanding help.

But who would come? The EOD was gone.

"Don't do this to me, Dylan," Rachel begged him. Her gun was on the dock, near her knees. Her hands were hard on his wounds. "You stay with me, you got that? You *stay with me.*"

His eyelids flickered. She saw the darkness of his gaze for a moment. It fixed on her.

"Love…" he rasped.

"I love you," Rachel told him, leaning close, desperate now. "And you're going to be with me for fifty more years, got it? This isn't the end. You're a SEAL. SEALs are tough—"

His breath heaved out.

Noelle's hands joined Rachel's. They both put pressure on the wound. "The bullet tore right through him," Noelle said, voice ragged.

Rachel felt as if the bullet had torn through her. "You're the good guy," she said to Dylan, remembering their first meeting. "You promised to keep me safe. Keep that promise. You have to stay with me. That's the only way. You have to make sure that I'm safe—"

Because without him, Rachel thought she'd be lost.

His eyes tried to focus on her. "Safe…"

She nodded, too aware that tears were sliding down her cheeks.

"Hate…when you…cry…" he whispered.

"Dylan—"

His eyes widened. He was looking right over her shoulder. With a sudden strength that stunned her, Dylan pushed Rachel and Noelle back. She followed his gaze and saw that—

Kenneth stood on the dock, dripping water. His lip was bleeding, and a snarl twisted his mouth. His eyes were on Dylan. "I'll finish you!"

Kenneth leaped forward.

Dylan staggered to his knees. He was trying to shove Rachel behind him as he still attempted to protect her.

Only it was her turn to protect him.

She lifted her gun. Aimed.

Fired.

Kenneth stared at her with wide, stunned eyes. He glanced down. "Such…fighter…" His legs buckled.

Then his face slammed into the dock.

Rachel wrapped her arms around Dylan. "Now it's over."

Sirens screamed in the night.

Dylan shuddered against her.

"Hold on just a little longer," she told him. "Please…"

His hand lifted. Found hers. He had to be in agony but he said, "For you…always…"

Tires squealed. Doors slammed. Rachel looked over and saw what looked like a mini-army of vehicles in the harbor's lot.

Familiar vehicles. Those black SUVs were favored by one particular D.C. group.

The EOD.

Mercer jumped from the first vehicle. *Mercer?*

Rachel shook her head and held tighter to Dylan.

"We've got an injured agent! Get him a medic now!" Mercer thundered even as he ran to the dock.

He paused for just a second next to Kenneth's body. He bent, checked for a pulse. Disgust tightened his lips. "You got off easy," he muttered and he left the dead man.

Two medics swarmed Dylan. They took him from Rachel and loaded him onto a stretcher.

Mercer grabbed her hand. "I heard it all, Agent Mancini."

She shook her head. "How are you even here? The blast—"

"We were already out of the EOD when I got your call. I just didn't have time to tell you before the whole place went to hell." His jaw locked. "I remembered what Noelle said, about you being the thing the guy cared about the most, and he was so hell-bent on getting you out of there…"

She barely heard him. Rachel couldn't take her eyes off Dylan and the medics. *They were taking Dylan away.*

"When my instincts scream at me, you can believe that I listen to them." He moved, shifting his stance so that he blocked her view of Dylan. "My instincts about you and Agent Foxx were dead-on from the beginning."

She could only shake her head. She didn't even know what instincts the guy was talking about.

"I knew right from the start that Dylan Foxx would be willing to die to keep you safe."

She spared a glance for Kenneth's still body. *And I killed for him.* Her gaze went back to the person who mattered. She eased a bit to the side of Mercer so that she could clearly see Dylan.

The medics were about to take him away. "Sorry, Mercer, but he's not leaving without me." She raced to keep up with them as they left the dock.

Dylan was still conscious. She saw that as she neared

him. He was injured so badly, but he still reached out to her.

She caught his hand. Held tight.

"This won't...hold me back...for long..."

His words seemed to be a warning.

"When they...stitch me up..."

The medics loaded him into an ambulance.

"I get to...savor you..."

Her heart jerked in surprise. He hadn't just said—

He *had*.

"Takes more than this...to stop me..."

Yes, it did. Then, right in the middle of a nightmare, Rachel found herself laughing.

She knew then—Dylan was going to be just fine.

And so was she.

THE CABIN WAS SECLUDED, far away from any prying eyes. It sat at the top of the mountain, seemingly in the middle of the clouds. When Dylan stepped on the balcony, he inhaled a deep gulp of fresh air—and he thought about how quickly his life had changed.

He'd gotten out of the hospital after two days. Two damn long days. Rachel had been there to see him, staying close, because he needed her close by.

Mercer had been at the hospital, too. The boss had come in to update him on the EOD's efforts to apprehend the others who'd helped Kenneth bomb the EOD.

For now, Dylan wasn't working that particular case. He was on leave.

The door slid open behind him.

And I'm with Rachel.

He turned and glanced back at her. There would be no interruptions up here. No danger. No threats.

Just him. Just her. The way he wanted it to be.

Dylan lifted his hand toward her. Rachel smiled at him, a sweet, slow smile that started with the curve of her lips and ended with a gleam in her eyes.

She came to him with soft steps, and her fingers locked with his.

The cabin was his, an escape that he'd built years ago because he hadn't wanted his life to be only about blood and death. Rachel was the only woman he'd ever brought there.

Rachel was the only woman he ever wanted at his side.

She leaned up onto her tiptoes, and her lips brushed over his.

He stilled at the sensual touch, aware of a heavy surge of emotion within him. Did Rachel understand just how much she meant to him?

She eased away from him. "So this is where you snuck off to on those vacation days of yours. You left me behind in the city and—"

"I never want to leave you again." The words pushed up from deep inside.

Her eyes widened.

He should probably try to be suave about this. Be charming. But he wasn't the charming guy. He was a fighter, an agent and a man who would kill in an instant if it meant he could protect the woman he loved.

He still held her hand in his. Dylan glanced down at their hands as he tried to find the right words for her.

"For a few days," Rachel said, speaking softly, "why don't we just pretend that the rest of the world doesn't exist?"

Dylan shook his head. "I want more than a few days

with you." He wanted everything she had to give. In return, he'd give her all that he was. "It was never a charade for me, you know that, don't you?"

Her eyes searched his.

"I wanted you for years. Dreamed of you. Needed you." He swallowed. "Loved you."

"Dylan—"

He should probably be on one knee for this. Damn it, what was wrong with him? *Get on your knee, Foxx.* He slipped down, letting his knee hit the wood of the balcony.

"What are you doing?" Rachel demanded as she immediately tried to pull him right back up to his feet. "Your stitches! You're going to hurt yourself."

Doubtful. He could walk through fire then and barely feel the burn as long as she was with him.

He looked up at her. "I want you to marry me."

Her jaw dropped.

And he'd messed up. Said the wrong thing. *Try for charm.* "No." Dylan jerked his head quickly. "What I meant… Rachel, you're the best thing that has ever happened to me. The only woman I want. The woman that I love so much—" He heaved out a breath. "I love you so much I can't even think of being in this world without you."

Rachel was silent.

"I can't promise that things will be easy." They'd never had easy. "I can promise that I will *always* be there for you. I will love you every day of my life, and I will…" He tried to smile. "I will savor you every night."

"Dylan…"

"Please, Rachel, marry me?"

Her hand lifted. Stroked the side of his cheek. Her

soft palm rasped over the faint stubble that had grown there. "I love you."

He found that now *he* couldn't speak.

"You were the first light I saw…after I was kidnapped. You promised to take care of me, and you did. On missions, at home… I've never felt alone since I met you."

She would never be alone again. "Tell me that's a yes," he managed to say. Beg? With Rachel, he damn well wasn't too proud to plead.

She smiled and took away his breath. "It's definitely a yes."

He was on his feet in the next instant. His arms were wrapped tightly around her. His mouth crushed down on hers. Dylan lifted her up against him.

"No!" She'd torn her mouth from his. "I told you— your stitches—"

"Let them come out. Nothing is stopping me now."

Because he had the one thing that he'd wanted most. He wasn't letting her go.

Dylan carried her back inside. He kissed her, caressed her. Their clothes were tossed across the room, and then he had her spread out on the big bed.

Their fingers twined together. Their mouths met. She was the sweetest thing he'd ever tasted. The one woman he could not live without.

He kissed his way down her body. Had her moaning and twisting beneath him. He loved her breasts—so perfect and full. He licked her. He kissed.

He explored every inch of her body.

Her nails raked over him.

Good. She wasn't worrying about his stitches any longer.

Dylan positioned his body between her legs. He looked up and met her gaze.

He saw his future when he looked into Rachel's gleaming eyes. A future he'd only dreamed of before that moment.

He thrust into her.

She wrapped her legs around him and met him, thrust for thrust.

When the pleasure hit, it swept them both away. So intense that the world seemed to go dark.

He looked only at her—because to Dylan, she was all that mattered.

He kissed her once more.

He wouldn't live for the next mission any longer. From now on, Dylan knew he'd only be living…

For her.

Epilogue

Bruce Mercer stared up at the EOD building. The explosions could have been much worse. He could have lost a lot of good men and women.

All because someone wanted to kill me.

He knew the list of his enemies stretched far and wide. He'd always made waves in this world.

He glanced around at the wreckage. Two vehicles had been placed near the building. One in the front. One in the back. Loaded down with explosives. Set to go.

But his security personnel had noticed those vehicles as soon as they arrived. The EOD had cameras all along the street. *No* vehicles were ever allowed to park immediately near the building.

And in light of the fear that he'd already been feeling, red flags had gone off immediately when those cars arrived.

There were numerous exits from the EOD building. Not just those that the public saw. Getting his agents away from the building and away from those cars had been easy.

But his teams never had the chance to disarm the bombs. They'd gone off too quickly.

The men who'd driven those vehicles? *Dead.* His

agents had taken care of them. They'd tried to bring the men in alive, but, in the end, there hadn't been a choice.

"So…" The quiet voice came from right beside him. Noelle Evers turned to study him. "What are you going to do now?"

"The same thing I always do. Go after the bad guys." He'd find the man who'd paid Kenneth Cross.

And he had just the agent in mind for that job.

Thomas Anthony. The Dragon.

Noelle raised her brows as she studied him. "Does any of this ever affect you? Or have you really closed that much of yourself away?"

Ah, now he wouldn't reveal that, not even to her. "Don't profile me, Noelle," he warned her. "I don't think you'd like the man you find hidden inside."

She nodded. "Fair enough."

"But I do want you working on this case," he said, jerking his hand toward the scorched remains. "You and Thomas Anthony—you *will* find the man who did this. You'll find out what he cares about, where he hides—you will find out everything about him." He drew in a deep, shuddering breath. "And then we will destroy him."

Because no one got away with an attack like this.

You come after me…after my people—your mistake. Because the man behind this attack would be the one to pay.

* * * * *

COMING NEXT MONTH FROM

H HARLEQUIN®

INTRIGUE®

Available August 19, 2014

#1515 MAVERICK SHERIFF
Sweetwater Ranch • by Delores Fossen
Thrown into a dangerous investigation, Sheriff Cooper McKinnon and
Assistant District Attorney Jessa Wells must join forces to protect the baby
they each claim as their own.

#1516 WAY OF THE SHADOWS
Shadow Agents: Guts and Glory • by Cynthia Eden
FBI profiler Noelle Evers can't remember him...but former army ranger
Thomas Anthony would kill in order to protect the one woman he can't live
without. With Noelle once again in a predator's sights, can Thomas save
the woman he loves a second time?

#1517 DEAD MAN'S CURVE
The Gates • by Paula Graves
When CIA double agent Sinclair Solano is lured out of hiding to recover his
kidnapped sister, he crosses swords with a beautiful FBI agent, Ava Trent,
who wants him—dead or alive.

#1518 THE WHARF
Brody Law • by Carol Ericson
Police Chief Ryan Brody trusts true-crime writer Kacie Manning to help
him catch a killer, but Kacie is keeping a dark secret from him. Can Kacie
abandon her quest for revenge to give their love a chance...or will the *real*
psychopath get to her first?

#1519 SNOW BLIND
by Cassie Miles
After witnessing a murder, Sasha Campbell turns to local sheriff's deputy
Brady Ellis for protection. But while Brady and Sasha grow closer to one
another, the killer gets dangerously closer to them.

#1520 STALKED
The Men from Crow Hollow • by Beverly Long
Tabloid celebrity Hope Minnow believes recent death threats are a
publicity stunt and refuses navy intelligence officer turned bodyguard
Mack McCann's protection. But when the threats turn very real, can Mack
get to Hope in time to save her?

**YOU CAN FIND MORE INFORMATION ON UPCOMING HARLEQUIN® TITLES,
FREE EXCERPTS AND MORE AT WWW.HARLEQUIN.COM.**

HICNM0814

REQUEST YOUR FREE BOOKS!
2 FREE NOVELS PLUS 2 FREE GIFTS!

HARLEQUIN®
INTRIGUE®

BREATHTAKING ROMANTIC SUSPENSE

YES! Please send me 2 FREE Harlequin Intrigue® novels and my 2 FREE gifts (gifts are worth about $10). After receiving them, if I don't wish to receive any more books, I can return the shipping statement marked "cancel." If I don't cancel, I will receive 6 brand-new novels every month and be billed just $4.74 per book in the U.S. or $5.24 per book in Canada. That's a savings of at least 14% off the cover price! It's quite a bargain! Shipping and handling is just 50¢ per book in the U.S. and 75¢ per book in Canada.* I understand that accepting the 2 free books and gifts places me under no obligation to buy anything. I can always return a shipment and cancel at any time. Even if I never buy another book, the two free books and gifts are mine to keep forever.

182/382 HDN F42N

Name _____ (PLEASE PRINT)

Address _____ Apt. #

City _____ State/Prov. _____ Zip/Postal Code

Signature (if under 18, a parent or guardian must sign)

Mail to the **Harlequin® Reader Service:**
IN U.S.A.: P.O. Box 1867, Buffalo, NY 14240-1867
IN CANADA: P.O. Box 609, Fort Erie, Ontario L2A 5X3

**Are you a subscriber to Harlequin Intrigue books
and want to receive the larger-print edition?
Call 1-800-873-8635 or visit www.ReaderService.com.**

* Terms and prices subject to change without notice. Prices do not include applicable taxes. Sales tax applicable in N.Y. Canadian residents will be charged applicable taxes. Offer not valid in Quebec. This offer is limited to one order per household. Not valid for current subscribers to Harlequin Intrigue books. All orders subject to credit approval. Credit or debit balances in a customer's account(s) may be offset by any other outstanding balance owed by or to the customer. Please allow 4 to 6 weeks for delivery. Offer available while quantities last.

Your Privacy—The Harlequin® Reader Service is committed to protecting your privacy. Our Privacy Policy is available online at www.ReaderService.com or upon request from the Harlequin Reader Service.

We make a portion of our mailing list available to reputable third parties that offer products we believe may interest you. If you prefer that we not exchange your name with third parties, or if you wish to clarify or modify your communication preferences, please visit us at www.ReaderService.com/consumerschoice or write to us at Harlequin Reader Service Preference Service, P.O. Box 9062, Buffalo, NY 14269. Include your complete name and address.

HI13R

SPECIAL EXCERPT FROM

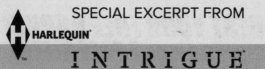

HARLEQUIN®

INTRIGUE®

*Thrown into a dangerous investigation,
Sheriff Cooper McKinnon and Assistant District
Attorney Jessa Wells must join forces to protect
the baby they each claim as their own.*

*Read on for an excerpt from MAVERICK SHERIFF
The first installment in the SWEETWATER RANCH series
by USA TODAY bestselling author Delores Fossen*

"You had my son's DNA tested, why?" Jessa demanded.
But that was as far as she got. Her chest started pumping
as if starved for air, and she dropped back and let the now
closed door support her.

The dark circles under her eyes let him know she hadn't
been sleeping.

Neither had he.

It'd taken every ounce of willpower for him not to rush
back to the hospital to get a better look at the little boy.

"How's Liam?" he asked.

She glared at him for so long that Cooper wasn't sure
she'd answer. "He's better, but you already know that. You've
called at least a dozen times checking on his condition."

He had. Cooper also knew Liam was doing so well that
he'd probably be released from the hospital tomorrow.

"He'll make a full recovery?" Cooper asked.

Again, she glared. "Yes. In fact, he already wants to get
up and run around. Now, why?" she added without pausing.

Cooper pulled in a long breath that he would need and
sank down on the edge of his desk. "Because of the blood
type match. And because we never found my son's body."

Even though she'd no doubt already come up with that

answer, Jessa huffed and threw her hands in the air. "And what? You think I found him on the riverbank and pretended to adopt him? Well, I didn't, and Liam's not your son. I want you to put a stop to that DNA test."

Cooper shook his head. "If you're sure he's not my son, then the test will come back as no match."

Her glare got worse. "You're doing this to get back at me." Her breath broke, and the tears came.

Oh, man.

He didn't want this. Not with both of them already emotional wrecks. They were both powder kegs right now, and the flames were shooting all around them. Still, he went closer, and because all those emotions had apparently made him dumber than dirt, Cooper slipped his arm around her.

She fought him. Of course. Jessa clearly didn't want his comfort, sympathy or anything else other than an assurance to put a stop to that test. Still, he held on despite her fists pushing against his chest. One more ragged sob, however, and she sagged against him.

There it was again. That tug deep down in his body. Yeah, dumber than dirt, all right. His body just didn't seem to understand that an attractive woman in his arms could mean nothing.

Even when Jessa looked up at him.

That tug tugged a little harder. Because, yeah, she was attractive, and if the investigation and accusations hadn't cropped up, he might have considered asking her out.

So much for that plan.

Find out what happens next in
MAVERICK SHERIFF
by USA TODAY *bestselling author Delores Fossen,*
available September 2014, only from
Harlequin® Intrigue®.

Copyright 2014 © by Delores Fossen

HIEXP69782

HARLEQUIN®

INTRIGUE

THE WOMAN WHO DOESN'T REMEMBER
IS THE ONE HE CAN'T FORGET IN THE
LATEST INSTALLMENT OF
NEW YORK TIMES BESTSELLING
AUTHOR CYNTHIA EDEN'S
SHADOW AGENTS: GUTS AND GLORY

Fifteen years ago, Noelle Evers was kidnapped. Two days
later, her abductor was dead, leaving her with no memory
of what happened. Now an FBI profiler, she uses her past
trauma to get inside the minds of killers. But she can't
read her new partner. EOD agent Thomas Anthony is
controlled. Dangerous. And hauntingly familiar.

Thomas has been covertly watching Noelle's back. He
wanted to tell her the truth, but couldn't blow his cover.
Their latest mission just revealed a link to her past. With
desire ramping up between them—and a predator hunting
Noelle—it's time for Thomas to step out of the shadows.
Or lose his second chance to save the woman he loves.

WAY OF THE SHADOWS

BY CYNTHIA EDEN

Only from Harlequin® Intrigue®.
Available September 2014
wherever books and ebooks are sold.

—— www.Harlequin.com ——

HI69783